# THE GHOST KILLERS OF
# BLACK ASH CANYON

## WILLIAM KERRIGAN

ISBN 978-1-942946-00-7

To my mother, Barbara Dawn Kerrigan,
who wanted me to tell stories.

CHAPTER ONE

On a hot day in August I had just escaped Santa Barbara's noontime traffic and was zipping north on California 101. I passed through lazily unwinding cattle ranches and tightly ordered vineyards. Between hills I caught fleeting glimpses of the high peaks surrounding the Santa Ynez Valley. I was on my way to . . . well, a place to live, a place to start over. Where was a serious secret.

I grew up in San Luis Obispo County, the only child of Lauren and Gregory Buckman, owners and managers of a small country inn nestled among prosperous horse farms in the valleys to the east of Paso Robles. They named me Michael after my mother's beloved father. I hardly knew the man, who died in my third year. The main grandfather in my life was Wilbur Buckman, who dealt in art and antiques, wrote travel books, and lived long enough to pass on to me some of the old-fashioned graces.

As a boy I worked in our stables or assisted our chefs, then later on helped plan horseback picnic outings to nearby fishing streams and hilltop viewing areas. I knew where our guests could catch a trout or behold eagles and condors circling in the high winds. My unspoiled kingdom was bordered on the west by touristy beach communities (San

Simeon, Cambria, Cayucos, Morro Bay) and on the east by the hot inland farming towns of Paso Robles (where I was schooled), Templeton, Atascadero, and San Luis Obispo.

All of those little towns, in my youth, had dying movie theatres where old-timers could get out of the heat, shiver deliciously in the frozen air emitted by rickety old air-conditioning units turned all the way down, watch a double bill of second-run features, and bankrupt themselves buying ridiculously overpriced lobby food. Youngsters went there on dates. My grandfather, who welcomed movies with a simple unaffected joy, took me as a child. Later, I went to the local theaters whether I had a date or not. By the time I graduated from high school I had gathered a library from used bookstores and thrift shops with titles such as *American Directors, The Biographical Dictionary of Cinema, Cinema Stylists, What is Cinema?* and *The Imaginary Signifier.* My native turf had a lot to offer. But I yearned for neon marquees and thriving revival houses. Whenever our family vacations would take us to a real city, the first thing I wanted to do was visit their gaudiest downtown movie palaces.

My parents had both been raised in Virginia. With their blessing I attended the University of Virginia, then entered the graduate film program at Columbia University. New York was my idea of heaven. To this day I believe that there is no better place in the world for a serious filmgoer. Where else can you attend a late night double bill of *Diary of a Country Priest* and *Les dames du Bois de Boulogne* at the Film Forum and run into a sobbing Woody Allen in the men's room? But California was in my blood. After taking a Master's at Columbia, I landed a job at the American Film Institute in Hollywood, where I labored for four years on one of those vast pious research missions that paralyze the finances and human energies of institutions such as the AFI more often than outsiders realize. We were gradually publishing encyclopedic catalogs containing the most accurate information ever assembled about the release dates, production details, box-office performance, and archived prints of all American films from 1909 to 2000.

The series had adopted the standard format of one volume for each year. It generally took a little more than a year to prepare one of these books. A generation of young AFI film scholars had gone gray setting the historical record straight for 1909 to 1935. That's when I came aboard. I contributed about a quarter of the information for the catalogues covering 1936, 1937, and 1938.

The work was somewhat rewarding. Old high school friends, now selling Porches or building internet businesses in the Third World, understood the project. It was virtuous, a gift to the future's understanding of twentieth-century American movies. It might, it *would* change some of the mistaken assumptions of film history. It would be used and cited. Mine was one of five names listed on the title pages of our books, and it's always impressive to have a "Publications" section in your résumé. Joe Kennedy made sure that his well-prepared son could claim authorship of something called *Profiles in Courage*, though it was ghost-written from beginning to end by Ted Sorenson.

But in other ways the work was dull and dulling. Beneath the respect shown this enterprise by family, friends, and colleagues, deep pools of contempt and derision simmered. "Really?" you could almost hear them thinking, "You're wasting your life on *that*?" The world's instincts usually have something to be said for them. These were books few private individuals would choose to purchase. They were sold by and large to specialty film libraries at colleges and universities. No one would ever read them in the usual sense. They were consulted for the specs on a particular film or group of films, and users would never look through our entries for anything bearing on the meaning or import of a particular movie.

The senior editor in our pack of five was a dedicated pedant named Edmund Webb. He and I fought long tiring battles over many of my draft entries. I privately dubbed him Jackass Webb, since his main advice to the research team was "Just the facts, Ma'am," as Sgt. Friday (or actor Jack Webb) used to tell emotional interviewees on the old *Dragnet* television show. Occasionally I won, persuading Jackass to allow me a couple of insightful sentences on the miniature screwball comedy embedded in the subplot of an early William Boyd western or how films set in the South Seas often drew on the atmosphere of gothic melodramas. Not that reviewers ever noticed these grace notes. They didn't read the books either.

Looking back now, I realize that Webb had the right idea. The reason I cared so much about peppering the entries with critical insights was that I myself could not live with the intellectual vacuity of these maddeningly factual volumes. Ours was a virtuous drudgery that the AFI funded every year, one proud budget after another, but no one in the film world considered the least bit interesting or exciting. Sandra Bullock's gardener had more glamour than I did, and was no doubt more envied than I was.

It was not, however, four years of trampling out the vintage where the Gripes of Ennui are stored that led me to quit my Hollywood job and move to a remote canyon in northern Santa Barbara County with the vague thought of writing a novel, a screenplay, a memoir, *something*. I was running from the failure of my marriage.

I'll give you a brief run-down. I had been asked to participate in a panel discussion after an event at the AFI theater. One of our archivists had discovered a beautiful print of an early talkie called *Reaching for the Moon* in an empty swimming pool behind a crumbling mansion on the outskirts of Toronto. The film starred Douglas Fairbanks and Bebe Daniels, with a debut appearance by the young Bing Crosby, and was based on an idea by Irving Berlin. Critics had often complained that the movie contained only one Berlin song, given of course to Crosby and then reprised by Daniels. But the new print was fifteen minutes longer than any other known, and contained two musical numbers that, as had long been suspected, were filmed but eventually trimmed from release copies. One of these new numbers featured a brief section of Crosby and Fairbanks singing and dancing together.

When my turn came to address the audience after the showing, I remarked on how the muscular Fairbanks and the narrow-shouldered Crosby, different in obvious ways, shared a physical comfort before the camera, a kind of animal indifference to the thrill of being recorded. I contrasted this "naturalness" to the self-conscious star turns of Bebe Daniels.

I think my remarks were well received by the audience, but the last speaker on our panel, an ambitious young producer named Carolyn Nast, stole both my thunder and the show.

She began by praising my comments on how Fairbanks presented his body to the camera. Still, she speculated, Fairbanks only seemed relaxed and natural because he had been imitated, whether consciously or not, by generations of leading men. She concentrated on a scene in *Reaching for the Moon* where the star, having taken a love potion, becomes frenetically hyper-active. This was his true legacy: to shift from relaxed nonchalance to extreme physical exertion without forfeiting the illusion of naturalness. She compared Fairbanks to Errol Flynn, then Tony Curtis, Burt Lancaster, Kirk Douglas, Steve McQueen, Clint Eastwood, Sylvester Stallone, Tom Cruise, and others in the Fairbanks line, showing how each of them had incorporated gestures of their own, appealing to new generations of film viewers, while keeping in touch with the Fairbanks heritage, particularly his ability to shift from a kind of lazy but potent stillness to desperate exertion. She wound up speaking of her own aims as a producer. Miss Nast wanted to find young actors in the Fairbanks mold and mate them with parts as perfect for their biological energies as Robin Hood, Zorro, the Thief of Bagdad, the Black Pirate, and D'Artagnon had been for their great original.

I loved her braininess, but was put off at first by the strict, mannish cut of her brunette hair, as geometrical as a Bauhaus apartment. I did discern a cuteness signal in the white plastic frames of her glasses, backed up by possibly buxom swells inside her business suit.

After our presentation, over cocktails in the lounge next to the theater, I asked her to dinner. We hit it off. I began accompanying Carolyn to parties, premieres, and charity functions. I was right about the buxom swells. Our sex life was spectacular, and I was pleased to learn that she didn't need drugs to fuel her passions. My fellow researchers razzed me about my appearances in newspaper accounts of Hollywood social life. But glamour, tricky to gain and treacherous to keep, was the right thing to have in this town. Jackass Webb began to give in to my brief attempts to assess the meaning and importance of the films in our catalog. Carolyn's friends became my friends. I read the scripts she was considering, and gave my opinion on their strengths and pitfalls. I was present at some of her interviews with young players. Entertainment reporters from print and television noted me.

Her father, who specialized in importing British stage properties to Broadway, americanizing their stories and sometimes transforming them into musicals, had died a few years back. But her mother, the formidable Sally Nast, carried on his work. Carolyn and I flew to New York to see Sally's latest musical based on a Trollope novel. The next night she hosted a small dinner party for us, and at the end served a lavish chocolate layer cake that had once upon a time, she revealed when the guests were gone, won her husband's heart. She approved of me. Three months later Carolyn and I married at a villa on Catalina Island owned by one of her actress friends. I moved into her home in Brentwood.

She offered me an executive position in her production company. In retrospect, I should probably have accepted. But at the time I thought it prudent to keep our careers separate. My new cachet in the world of contemporary moviemaking gave me hope for advancement at the AFI. At a Hollywood party a member of the Institute's Board of Directors told me that I was being considered for an appointment as a Research Scholar. That had been my ambition throughout my time at Columbia. I had never been interested in producing or directing. I wanted to be a major film historian. As a Research Scholar, I would have a trailer to myself on the AFI campus with my own secretaries, free to shape my own projects in film history and criticism. It was like being a college professor without the obligation to teach students. In the hope of occupying such a desirable position, I elected to stay at the AFI.

It didn't happen overnight. They kept me working on the catalog. It took us two years to finish the 1939 volume, which might turn out to be the crown jewel of the entire project. 1939, which saw the releases of *Gone with the Wind*, *The Wizard of Oz*, *Gunga Din*, *Stagecoach*, *Ninotchka*, *Only Angels Have Wings*, *The Women*, *Mr. Smith Goes to Washington*, and many more, was widely considered to be the jubilee year of American film studio production, and of all the volumes published so far in our make-work project, this one stood the best chance of being noticed. I was winning almost all my battles with Jackass at that point. In fact, we rarely battled at all any more. Webb would glance through my copy, shake his head disapprovingly, sigh, and OK the entry. I was also allowed to sign the entries I wrote, rather than, as in previous volumes, leaving the peculiar impression that all five of the editors had somehow written everything. Just over two years into my marriage I was promoted to Research Scholar.

Within months I began two books. The first was an exploration of Fairbanks and the tradition of heroism in American action films. This book was of course rooted in my relationship with Carolyn. Our initial meeting of minds had been good for her. She bought the rights to the Steve McQueen movie *Bullitt*, and worked in close concert with a team of scriptwriters to update the story, the character, the car—even the city. An internet search revealed that the hilliest metropolis in the world was not San Francisco, but La Paz, Bolivia. She set the script there, and found a young Hispanic actor to play the McQueen role. We tossed some titles around. *Magnum Bullitt. Bullitt Point. Live Bullitt. Bullitt in Bolivia.* Finally some rising star at Nast Productions, a certain Leonard DeForrest, late of the film school at USC, had the idea of naming our south-of-the-border McQueen "Aurelio Ammo" and calling the movie *Gold Ammo.* The hero has an affair with a rich American ex-pat, who, the first time they fall into bed together, says, in a languorous sexual tone, "I've heard of the The Man with the Golden Arm and The Man with the Golden Gun, but I never dreamed I would have Gold Bullets in my vaginal barrel! It's like Zeus and Danae." Some of the early reviewers, praising the unusual literacy of the film's script, explained the classical allusion, and the line became one of that day's in-things to know about. It was always greeted in theaters with a thick wave of knowing titters. The movie was a big hit, and Carolyn followed it with *Gold Ammo Reloaded* and *Pot of Gold Ammo*, which did even better at the box-office, especially in Central and South America.

Though we discussed casting and script revisions, I mostly kept my distance from Carolyn's movies. The one main exception was a little horror film. An old friend of hers, Vicky Enders, had optioned a script called *Fog-Bound* and asked Carolyn to co-produce it on a small budget. One evening, when my wife was out at a dinner party with a group of female producers and directors, I read through the script.

It was no great shakes. Basically the film was an update of *The Exorcist* without the Catholic trappings. A paranormal investigator in northern California agrees to help a family whose youngest son seems to have been invaded by an otherworldly entity who might be trying to destroy the child, or might be trying to destroy the family through the child. There is often a logic of sacrifice at the bottom of horror films. Someone must die, or must be seriously changed, in order for the supernatural threat to be defused. In this case the investigator, like a primitive shaman, is able to absorb the demonic entity and free the suffering family, but at the cost of a portion of his soul. The script hinted, though not very effectively, that the tortured family were never flesh-and-blood to begin with, but spectral projections of the demon or ghosts, whose target all along was the paranormal investigator himself.

On impulse I began fiddling with the movie, adding a new scene clarifying the intent of the demon and a final scene pointing more specifically toward the lost aspects of the investigator's personality. The project, in my handling of it, ended with the struggle against the demon becoming a lifelong struggle within the investigator's psyche. Both Carolyn and Vicky were enthusiastic about my additions, and offered me a screenwriting credit. I refused that honor, but the film was made with my modifications. *Fog-Bound* broke even in the theaters, but turned a nice profit in its DVD release. It acquired a small yet vocal following, and is still discussed occasionally by horror-buff bloggers and forums.

While my wife became the hottest young producer in town, I quickly lost interest in the Fairbanks project. I started gathering materials for a book on the peculiar effect of mental illness on the performances of certain actresses. You could see the beginning of a template in Garbo. But Judy Garland was my archetype. Increasingly in her career, the implicit threat of breakdown or even suicide made a kind of unconscious pact with the audience. Fans could fend off that threat, *temporarily*, by wildly valuing her current performance. Their excessive applause, their slightly too laudatory word of mouth, saved her life for the time being. But of course the same audiences, having the power to give life, have the power to end it. I wrote a long section on how complexly this game was played in her movies. For example, her various implicit pacts with the audience sometimes mirrored and sometimes undermined similar arrangements with her gay husband and sometime director, Vincente Minnelli. I followed the Garland discussion with a detailed analysis of Gene Tierney and Jennifer Jones. There was a chapter on Marilyn Monroe and the sexualizing of Garland's classic moves, with asides on the doomed queen of late B-quality noirs, Barbara Payton. I wanted to end with Demi Moore in films like *The Scarlet Letter*, *Disclosure*, and *Indecent Proposal.* I also had thoughts about Gwyneth Paltrow. Really, I had too many thoughts. I was channel surfing one night and ran into a reality television program about Ryan and Tatum O'Neal. Before long Tatum's childhood roles seemed a perfect extension of my thesis.

In the end, the fear of lawsuits led me to follow the advice of Carolyn's legal team and write a brief final chapter mentioning Moore, Paltrow, and O'Neal, along with a few other living actresses, while covering my ass with words like "perhaps" and "possibly." I was grateful but not overly so when Simon and Schuster agreed to publish *Adoration or Else: Disturbed Actresses and Their Audience.* I knew it was good. I believed it would sell.

It took me three years to write the book. During this time Carolyn suffered her first failure. Returning to a project that her father had toyed with for twenty years, she produced *An Aye for an Aye*, a rock 'n roll adaptation of Shakespeare's *Measure for Measure* set in an Arizona border town. Its failure left her sulking. But she bounced back, as I was finishing *Adoration or Else*, with a deft biopic about the young Mae West. *Sex Broad* put her on top again, and there was enough left of West's life to support two sequels.

As the book progressed, it absorbed more and more of my time. I had no explanation for why people close to me, especially my secretary Gale Durling, began directing furtive pitying glances at me as I prepared my computer files for publication. If I thought about it at all, I supposed they anticipated failure, or on the contrary were sad that success might elevate me beyond their sphere.

One overcast afternoon I wrote the final paragraph. I used a word that I had trotted out three pages before. I went back and changed to another, wanting to save that word's full virginal power for the last page. I removed a comma from a neighboring sentence. I changed out a stiff phrase for an idiomatic one. I read it over. At least for now, it was finished.

I gave Gale the afternoon off, slipping her a hundred dollar bonus from my own wallet. She thanked me, and as her eyes turned slowly toward the door, I sensed a tender regret. Did she fear I was moving on to greater things, leaving her with a new boss or no job at all? I had other things on my mind.

I stopped off at a swank liquor store for a bottle of real French champagne. When I pulled up to my home in Brentwood, I was pleased to see Carolyn's car parked in the front courtyard. When I bounded into the bedroom Fairbanks-style, however, I was not at all pleased to see Brenda's lips savoring the veiny cock of her indispensable assistant Leonard DeForrest. There were neat lines of white powder on top of my bureau.

"Sorry, Mike. I really am. This isn't as personal as it seems. We're celebrating. Disney just bought *Sex Broad 2* for a hundred million!"

"Not personal? Right, I can see that. That's why you made my bureau into a coke caddy."

"Mike! Please. . . ."

No thanks, darling. I moved out that afternoon.

Within a week I realized that rumors of her sexual adventures had been flying around Hollywood for years. This is probably the part of my marriage you remember. The entertainment press opened their Carolyn Nast files, and affair after affair tumbled into tabloids and broadcasts. She became "Nasty Nast," and I, Mike Buckman, became "Mike the Cuckman." Funny, no? Everyone had their own story. Colleagues at the UFI would approach me with long-cherished tales of her legendary infidelities. Gale cried as she told me hers. She had been terribly worried about how these facts would impact me and my work. But now at last she revealed her infidelity news, framed by her deep concern for my welfare. One weekend, when Carolyn was supposedly meeting with a film composer in San Francisco, she was actually strutting her stuff on the Sausalito houseboat of my AFI nemesis Ed Webb. A bartender recognized my picture from some entertainment news program and told me one I had never heard before about Carolyn's late night meeting with a famous Hispanic movie star, "the guy in that brass bullet movie." One afternoon Carolyn's former shrink called me to apologize that professional discretion had kept him from alerting me to her self-destructive addictions. He subtly let me know that her determination to seduce him had led to an impasse in their therapeutic journey.

For years, apparently, I had been the most famous and worried over cuckold in Hollywood. And now I knew it. Funny, no?

I had to get out of the place. I surprised Carolyn and delighted her lawyers by setting aside my right to a 50-50 community property settlement, and agreeing to keep my car, a Lotus that she had given me for our fifth anniversary, 10% of the value of the house, and 15% of the value of her production company, in the belief that my advice had played a small roll in her success.

I soon found myself with a new book in print. The reviews had been favorable, and initial sales were strong, thanks in part to the notoriety of my recent divorce. Carolyn arranged to buy back my percentage of her production company. My ex-wife had gotten a very cheap divorce, but I had enough money in the bank to last a lifetime, and my agent was handling a stream of callers eager to give me an advance on my next book.

I had other ideas. I wanted to be under the radar, off the grid, and lost in space.

The AFI granted my request for an indefinite leave of absence with no pay. I arranged for a voice-mail drop so that my agent, financial advisor, and some few select friends and relatives could contact me electronically. I didn't want anyone, anyone at all, to know where I would be. My parents acknowledged my failed marriage with phone calls and a short visit to Los Angeles. They had felt excluded from my marriage, and now seemed resigned to playing a peripheral role in its destruction.

That must have been my hidden intention all along. What did the Great Buckman need from parents? Did he really have parents? With close to full independence at AFI, cocooned in money and insider knowingness through my marriage to Carolyn, I had allowed fantasies of self-authorship to take control of my life. Perhaps the experiment started with my insistence on an East Coast education. Perhaps it had started way before that, with my childhood passion for movie theaters and the brief illusion of self-sufficiency they provided. Before I could return to an ordinary personal life I yearned to spend time with absolute strangers, people who had never conquered me or been conquered by me, whose plans had never impinged on mine. I wanted a purer look at life's possibilities than I had ever before allowed myself.

I spent weeks on the internet looking for a wilderness cabin between San Luis Obispo and Goleta. The swanky movie theaters found in cities were not the routes to ecstasy I had imagined them to be, but flashy water slides that dropped you into the vast cess pool of a corrupt industry. I yearned for the quiet mountains and valleys of coastal California where I had grown up, but with one key difference: I wanted to be initially anonymous, which ruled out the Paso Robles area.

I found some possibles, checked them out, and made my decision. I put my belongings into storage, save for my oldest clothes, supplemented with a few new items I found in a farm supply warehouse and a store devoted to country and western gear. My upbringing had taught me fundamental prudence. So I applied for a permit to carry and bought a pistol, which I duly collected after the ten day waiting period. I sold the beautiful but fragile Lotus and purchased a two-year-old Dodge pickup with a supercharged V-8.

Everything in order, I drove the 101 through the mountain passes north of Goleta. I saw signs for the Danish settlement of New Aarhus. I zoomed by Lassiter Springs, home of the Green Troll Resort, serving the Green Troll Company's famed cheese-and-broccoli soup that I had been seeing on billboards for hours. My exit was just ahead.

I turned off at Las Sombras, drove through its handsome streets thick with art galleries and wine-tasting shops. Were there real people living in those second floor spaces above the gingerbread porch railings? The town seemed like the movie set of a civilized western village where nice girls brewed tea and took care of their fathers in comfortable homes behind picket fences, preparing box lunches to be raffled off, along with their companionship, at the monthly church social. It balanced this fantasy somewhat that there was not a movie theater in sight.

Leaving Las Sombras, I headed for the hills.

CHAPTER TWO

Cortina Hills Road led through the residential section of Las Sombras until reaching the shadows of the hills to the east of town, then wound south past the city schools to a park shaded by the massive twisting branches of ancient oaks. There the road became narrow, almost too narrow for double traffic, and poorly paved with unattended piles of crumbling white rock broken off from ledges above. A yellow sign told you to honk before turns. You did well to notice it, for there was not another. Just beyond that a rusting plaque wired to the top of a leaning aluminum pole announced that Cortina Hills Road had just become Black Ash Canyon Pass.

I knew from studying internet maps that the mouth of Black Ash Canyon was no more than a hundred yards wide. The road wound along the side of Mt. Sombras. The canyon floor was too heavily wooded to reveal signs of human habitation. I caught glimpses of what appeared to be a stream bed on the far edge. In this part of the state the vast cattle ranches of yesteryear were gradually morphing into vineyards. But no force on earth could transform the plunging V of this canyon into a simulacrum of Tuscany's rolling hills.

Around a corner, at the top of a sloping mound joining the two sides of the canyon, I came upon a small cemetery. A gray-haired woman in a straw bonnet and what looked to be a light blue cotton dress with a print of small flowers was standing before a gravestone just beyond the shadow line. A handsome palomino grazed in the sunlight between us. Because the road turned sharply just ahead, I honked. Out of the corner of my eye I saw the startled horse shy back into the shadows. I did not think the woman budged at all.

Gradually the valley floor widened until the canyon walls were approximately five hundred yards apart. I was traveling west. Twenty-five miles of canyon lay ahead. I knew that it would broaden continuously as the bordering mountains dwindled to hills, then turn to the south, opening into a small flat valley of choice farmland well able to support the usual truck crops in this part of California—lettuces, squashes, broccoli, strawberries. Eventually Black Ash Canyon Pass would empty into a main artery into Lassiter Springs. The canyon was divided up into five properties, one after another like the segments of a caterpillar. I was looking for the first of them, comprising the forbidding terrain of the canyon's initial five miles.

I passed a level area cut into the mountain's steep ascent. There was a turn-out there. Above a line of brush I saw the iron head of a donkey pump nodding up and down in its slow repeating manner. Someone, years back, had sunk an oil well in Black Ash Canyon. If there was one well successful enough to be still producing today, there would be others. Around the next bend was another ledge and another turn-out with a donkey relentlessly squeezing the last dregs of treasure from what was probably, a century ago, a small but promising oil field. Across the way, on the far side of the canyon, I noticed another mark of California history: a hole in the face of orange rock. Before oilers had sunk their wells, miners had dug their tunnels. Such signs of the past were familiar to me from my native stomping grounds outside of Paso Robles. The coastal wildernesses of California had been well and truly raped by men highly dedicated to the task.

The road descended rapidly until it was only twenty feet above the canyon floor. An unmarked dirt track peeled off the main road. This looked to be my destination. It led to a simple ranch gate, two fifteen-foot posts with a thick board nailed between them. Screwed to the center of the crossbeam was a rusty iron cutout in inch-thick letters reading GRIS-WOLD RANCH. Barbed-wire fencing extended in both directions. A bank of three mailboxes stood to one side. On the galvanized aluminum gates inside the wooden frame was a cluster of redundant signs reading "No Visitors Allowed," "Posted," "No Trespassing," "Keep Out," and "Violators Will Be Prosecuted." Off on one edge, commenting on these messages, was a shield-shaped sign. "Security by Smith and Wesson," it said.

As per my emailed instructions, I opened the gates and drove through, got out of the truck and closed them behind me, then continued on the dirt road beneath a shaded canopy of oaks, sycamores, and maples. Two hundred yards away in a cleared area pierced by the early afternoon sun stood a weathered red barn, a system of corrals, and a newish light orange adobe farm house with a green metal roof. A Mercedes SUV and new Ford truck were parked before a separate garage—both white, like my Dodge.

A tall white-haired man, perhaps in his early seventies, came out onto the front porch and down a brick path to greet me. He was dressed, as I was, in jeans and a cotton plaid shirt, but he also wore a straw-woven cowboy hat. I would have to buy myself a hat.

"Mike Buckman?"

"Yes, sir. You must be Ben Griswold."

"You chose a hot day to arrive. Come on in the house. Coffee will be ready in a minute or two. Maybe you would prefer a beer?"

"Coffee will be fine, thank you."

I entered a comfortable living room with a river-rock fireplace at one end and a bank of built-in shelves. While

Ben Griswold disappeared into the kitchen to serve our coffee, I looked over the items on display. Lots of Louis L'Amour paperbacks, Manchester's biography of Churchill, a smattering of best-selling history and fiction from the last forty years. There was only one book on movies, an older edition of Leonard Maltin's guide. On the walls were signed photos of horses decked out in fancy tack at various parades and celebrations. At the end of one of the bottom shelves I found a pile of plastic-encased *Wings* comic books from the 1940s.

"My father liked those," Ben said, setting a tray with two cups of coffee, a sugar bowl, and a pitcher of cream on a large wooden table before his leather couch.

"My grandfather Wilbur liked them, especially the Ghost Squadron tales. Do you collect old comics?"

"Not really. I don't collect anything. But I get these sudden spurts of interest. I bought that bunch last year from a store in Santa Barbara."

While we were chatting, I heard a sliding door open at the back of the house. An attractive dark-eyed woman entered the room in jeans and a Commander Cody tee-shirt, her brown hair pulled up in a soft ponytail. I couldn't help but notice that Commander Cody had never looked better.

"This is my daughter Cheyenne. We call her Shy, though she isn't. Shy, this is our new boarder, Mike Buckman."

I rose and shook her hand.

"Did you get the fence fixed?" Ben asked.

"I did, and had time to exercise Dark Star." It was clear that something was on her mind. "Do you know where Mom is? She's not in her room."

"I was working on that saddle for Del Packard. I couldn't find her when I broke for lunch. I was hoping she had gone for a walk."

Shy shook her head. "Paleface isn't in the barn. I'm afraid she took him out again."

Ben turned to me. "Sorry to bother you with this, Mike. We have to keep an eye out for my wife Valentina. Her memory fades in and out. The doctor hasn't said 'Alzheimer's' yet, but no one expects the condition to get better. Sometimes she forgets how to do things, like cook or clean or wash. Other times her memory for doing things is just fine, but she forgets people and places. Even me and Shy. Then again, she has good days, when everything is good and like it used to be. But when she rides out all by herself on her horse, I get worried."

"I think I may have seen her. A trim woman in a cotton dress with a palomino? I saw her at the grave—"

I was interrupted by a firm knock on the front door. Ben and Shy looked at each other for a moment, then both got to their feet. Something about the mood in the room made me stand up with them. Shy and I hung back a few steps while Ben opened the door.

It was the woman from the graveyard with a sparkle in her green eyes and a sweet quiet about her face. She looked up at Ben, blinking. A small smile curled the corners of her mouth and brought out the fine lines in her amber cheeks.

"*Perdóname, señor.* Sorry to bother you. I'm not sure where I am. I'm not sure I'm alive. Are you people alive? Are you living in this nice house?"

Shy stepped forward. "I'll take her, Dad." She walked her mother into the house and down a corridor leading, presumably, to the older woman's bedroom.

"Every day's an adventure," Ben said, as we returned to the leather couch. "Some days she remembers everything, even a little more than everything, adding  memories of things I just don't recall. Some days she forgets everything, including being alive."

"That's a big thing to forget."

"It is. But maybe we ought to get down to business."

He reached into his pocket and handed me the key to Shady Grove Cabin, which I had rented from him over the internet, paying him in advance for the first three months. He told me where it was—up by the road, about fifty yards before the main gate, hidden by surrounding trees. I had passed it without noticing on my way in. I sensed that he was politely giving me an out. I could leave this house of misery and begin my new life in Black Ash Canyon without being further burdened with his private sorrows. But I also sensed that the old man wanted to talk.

I asked about the history of the ranch. As the story tumbled out, I learned that Griswold Ranch and his marriage to Valentina were intertwined stories.

In 1848, when the Treaty of Guadalupe Hidalgo ended the Mexican-American War and formalized the annexation of California, Black Ash Canyon was a stretch of unwanted, unclaimed land between four large Mexican land-grant ranchos, the smallest of them over 30,000 acres. The Gold Rush of the ensuing years never really touched Santa Barbara Country. Mines were dug, and gold was rumored to have been found. But nothing was ever taken from the hills in this area of the state but quicksilver, gypsum, magnesia, and asphaltum.

Records were scarce. But it seemed that Black Ash Canyon was not only no man's land, but badlands, a refuge for fugitives and desperadoes of all stripes. The canyon was also an ideal place for rustlers to hide cattle stolen from the surrounding rancheros. According to modern title searchers (and Ben would have occasion to hire some of the best) the first owner of the canyon was the Southern Pacific Railway, which came through this area when building the long-delayed link from San Francisco to Santa Barbara. In repayment for this selfless act, the Southern Pacific received two hundred yards of land along its tracks, and every other section of land (640 acres) on both sides of the tracks, plus several square sections surrounding its stations. They put a station in the middle of nowhere close to the absolute nowhere of Black Ash Canyon and called it Las Sombras. Eventually a town would arise there.

In 1906 the Southern Pacific sold the canyon to United Oil. The oil industry had enjoyed considerable success in Southern California, and hoped to continue northward along the coast. The Sunderland field below Santa Barbara was an encouraging start. There was oil in Goleta too. In 1901 Union Oil struck it rich in Orcutt, and the "Old Maud" well sunk in 1904 became the premiere gusher in American oil history, pumping 12,000 barrels a day. The Santa Maria

Valley Field followed soon after. In 1908 the large Cat Canyon Field opened just to the southeast of Orcutt. United Oil hoped to duplicate these nearby successes in Black Ash Canyon. They sunk some wells, and they were profitable for a few years, but most of them eventually petered out or became diluted with sand and water.

Ben's uncle, Lars Griswold, purchased the first five miles at the mouth of the canyon from United Oil in 1925. Along with the property he inherited some agreeable squatters, a Spanish-Mexican couple named Angel and Consuela Acosta, who lived in a building now known as Old Cabin. Ben took me to the front window and pointed it out, a small weathered structure with a sagging front porch, probably just a few rooms, almost invisible, until your eyes caught its dark outline, in a shaded area fifty yards from the ranch house. No one lived there now, but the Old Cabin held great meaning for the Griswolds. Valentina had been born there, the daughter of Consuela and Angel. I would be able to see the old place, Ben told me, from the front porch of Shady Grove Cabin.

The other original ranch buildings had burned down, eventually to be replaced by the modern home in which we now sat. Ben remembered his happy summers at the original Griswold Ranch. Consuela presided over the kitchen, pickling fruits and vegetables, adept at providing the waffles and fritters favored by the wifeless Uncle Lars. Angel had a valuable skill as well. In a small shop that had stood near today's barn he made hand-tooled saddles and horse tack with custom silver work. The ranchers in this part of California had always loved, and to this day continued to love, parades, annual celebrations, local rodeos, fairs, and horse shows—any chance to appear in public looking like one of the old soldier rancheros, given many acres of fine New World property by the grateful rulers of Spain and Mexico. Angel's custom saddlery was much prized by the well-to-do ranchers of the area.

There were more and more of them, too, as the giant ranches of the old days were parceled out and sold. To the east the old Rancho de Sombra Loma was purchased by a wealthy Ohioan named Amos Lassiter. During a prolonged drought Lassiter sold off 11,000 acres to the Danish Settlement Corporation, which built New Aarhus on the property. His heirs, subdividing most of the remaining ranch land, established the city of Lassiter Springs, which then attracted executives of the Farm Fresh Corporation with their Green Troll greenbacks. All the new landowners of Las Sombras, New Aarhus, Lassiter Springs and the surrounding countryside wanted their fancy saddlery as well. They had bought the dream, and the dream was history, and fine leather with gleaming silver adornments to dress prancing horses was their link to history. Ben had apprenticed himself to Angel during those precious teenage summers at the Griswold Ranch. Now in his early seventies, he still filled orders for custom tack and saddles. Although the work had dwindled to a trickle, Ben cared less these days about income than the satisfaction he got from practicing his craft.

Ben's father had been an insurance broker in Los Angeles. He expected his son to take up a kindred profession. But those summers in Black Ash Canyon lured Ben toward an older and rougher way of life. It was not the least of the attractions of this older life that he had fallen deeply in love with Valentina Acosta. They rode horses together, exploring the ranch and its surroundings. They delivered saddles together, and hung out with the children of their customers. They read the same books about California history. When Lars died in 1965, childless, he left the ranch to Ben. The property had been damaged. Four years before Ben inherited, a fire had burned the old homestead to the ground, killing both Consuela and Angel. With the loss of her parents and his uncle, the young couple felt adrift rather than rooted. But they married and put the pieces together as best they could.

The ranch itself had never been particularly profitable. Ben took over the custom saddlery trade. He began selling fine oak firewood to the local inns and hotels. He offered himself as a guide to hunters.

But the finances of the Griswold Ranch remained a bleak picture until a day in 1972 when Ben was visited by an affable representative of a small oil company based in a neighboring county, Obispo Petroleum. He offered to test the old wells drilled early in the century by United Oil. If they were still capable of a profitable output, he would install electrical pumpjacks, and share the profits with Ben on a fifty-fifty basis. In the end, five of the seven old wells on the Griswold Ranch were equipped with nodding donkeys. One of them—located in the first turn-out I had noticed driving in—became known as "Old Faithful," and regularly produced twelve barrels a day. Another—in the second turn-out on Black Ash Canyon Way—yielded nine to ten barrels a day, and was dubbed "Gravy Train." The other three eked along at six to eight barrels a day. All told, with oil at $70 a barrel, and the ranch's wells producing thirty barrels a day, Ben made around $1000 per diem and his financial woes were at an end. Or almost. When United Oil caught wind of the Obispo Petroleum deal, their lawyers launched a suit, claiming that Lars Griswold's original purchase of the ranch land had not included drilling rights.

That's where the high-class title searchers came into play. The suit dragged on for three years, and ignited a bitter dispute with Theo Steele, owner of the adjacent property to the west. Title searchers hired by Ben's legal team discovered that there had been a United Oil subdivision of Black Ash Canyon in 1915, with the expectation that the property, given its thin trickle of crude oil, would have to be sold in the near future. This survey had been defective. The stated area of what became the Griswold Ranch was not consistent with its western boundary. A half mile of property that had for decades been part of the Steele Ranch in fact belonged to Ben Griswold. Moreover, this strip of land contained two more wells suitable for pumpjacking.

Steele's lawyers joined the fray. Theo spent without restraint on his suit. He had married a Lassiter woman. The main branches of that once-prominent family had sold their California holdings and moved on to Hawaii and Samoa, where they became prominent players in local real estate development. Theo was just about all that was left of Lassiter influence in Santa Barbara County. He fought Ben's suit with the fury of a dispossessed aristocrat—and lost, leaving him more furious and more dispossessed.

Once the legal clouds had been cleared away, and money was pumping regularly into his bank account, Ben rebuilt the ravaged ranch house, adding a barn with a new workshop and a complex of corrals. He put up a first rental cabin, known as the Creekside Chalet. On the side of the canyon across from the road was a little stream called Outlaw Creek. Dry for most of the year, it only ran during the rainy season, which usually began in October. Creekside Chalet was built on a rise above the stream. It was now occupied by a long-time resident named Solly Barlow. Ben doubted that I would see much of him. He had once traveled the globe as a wildcat oil prospector. Now in his fifties, he had turned against the modern world with its surveillance machines, its constant insistence that citizens be healthy and upbeat, enthusiastic about its mind-numbing products and amusements. Solly was also predictably bitter about taxes. He had been living in the seclusion of Creekside Chalet for the past twenty years.

It had been a swell chat, but both of us were ready to wind things up for the day. I needed to go shopping, for one thing.

"So," Ben said, leaning back. "You're a good listener. Are you going to be a good tenant?"

"I'm neat. I keep my music down. I'm not more than normally curious. I keep to myself. Will that do?"

He started a laugh. "That'll do just fine. One thing, though. Do you smoke?"

"No."

"Maybe you plan to do some hiking and camping around here? You're certainly welcome to hike and camp. But be careful with fire. You know what the name means? Black Ash Canyon?"

"I wondered about that. No ash trees around here. I take it the name doesn't refer to trees?"

"No. The old Spanish rancheros called it Canon de Cenizas Negras, Canyon of Black Ashes. Don't let these big green oaks fool you. A large stand of dry old trees in a twenty-mile wind tunnel? This whole place"—he gestured to his surroundings—"is black ashes waiting to happen. It's a great big tinder box. I'm told the canyon has been burned out four or five times in the last century and a half. My uncle was lucky the fire that destroyed his barn and house didn't take the whole damn canyon."

"Four or five times in a century and a half? That's not so bad. I know a guy in LA who tells me to expect disaster to touch my life every seven years."

Outside and on my own, my number one priority was to lay in basic provisions. I had seen a fancy gourmet grocery in

Las Sombras, but figured Lassiter Springs would be more in line with the kind of stuff I needed just now.

First I took a quick look at Shady Grove Cabin. The photos posted on the internet had not lied. My shady cabin was neat and simple, a living room and kitchen in the front, a bedroom and bathroom in the back, with its own water well and septic tank. I had a gas stove top and oven, both running off an outside propane tank. My covered porch had serviceable patio furniture and a rusty Weber grill. There was one happy surprise. In place of the amateurish landscapes pictured on the internet were some pieces of modern art that I rather liked on first acquaintance.

I could have gone back to Las Sombras and caught the 101 there, but decided to drive through the rest of Black Ash Canyon Pass. This way, as a bonus, I got a good look at Theo Steele's place. The first part of the ranch was narrow and wooded like the Griswold spread, but the property soon tapered out into cultivated farmland. There was a collection of rusted tractors, seed planters, and harvesters along a dirt road leading to a large metal building. A battered sign declared that "Farm Equipment Repairs" were done inside. Beneath and to one side of that was another sign. There was no rust, no sign of wear, on this one. Against a black lacquer background its neon tubes spelled the words "Ghost Killers" with pale green fire. The neon was on, glowing proudly and pointlessly in the afternoon haze on a seldom traveled road. What the heck was Ghost Killers? A brand of chewing tobacco? A local beer?

There were larger and nicer farms as the canyon turned south and continued broadening, becoming more like a small valley. Finally coming to a real road, I turned east to Lassiter Springs.

It seemed a prosperous town, on the edge of upscale. Lassiter Springs was small though, population 5,500 according to a sign. But here was everything Las Sombras lacked. Motels, shopping centers, department stores, car dealerships, chain outlets, ordinary businesses selling ordinary goods and services. In the center of town, the Green Troll complex sprawled as it had in years past, with its hotel, restaurant, and of course its famous gift shop, selling Green and Greta Troll dolls, soft enough for petting, packs of marbles in the shape and color of green peas, and Green Troll Trip Excitement Books, with games, quizzes, rebuses, pictures to color, and other Green Troll family amusements intended to make antsy children more docile on the road. Once upon a time, accompanied by my parents, I had been one of those moody kids in the gift shop. A ghastly place, many would testify. Today, however, there were choices. Around this venerable establishment were modern buildings with clean-looking restaurants, even two micro-breweries. Out among the car dealerships was The Saddle Tramp, a restaurant famous for its old-timey rustic atmosphere and good beef. Lassiter Springs would have its uses in the year to come.

I found the biggest supermarket in town. There were lots of trucks in the parking lot. My Dodge Ram felt right at home. After a thorough shop, I found a passable straw hat in a neighboring hardware store. I topped off my gas tank and headed up the 101 to Las Sombras, repeating my earlier entry into Black Ash Canyon. But now the shadows along the hills were longer and darker. Though I figured there must be over two hours of daylight left, night came quickly to my steep, narrow portion of the canyon. I could barely make out the graveyard, and had to use my headlights to locate the gate to Griswold Ranch.

I went to work on the grill with my new wire brush and a couple of Brillo pads. Declaring it fit for use, I rubbed down a potato with olive oil and stuck it in the oven, then filled the Weber with a bed of briquettes and lit them. A hour later, having just put my seasoned steak on, I pushed back my new straw hat and sipped a scotch and soda. There was still light in the sky above the canyon. The westering sun was up there too, but muffled and filtered by overarching trees.

From one angle of the porch I could look up at the road fifty feet away and fifteen feet above me, or stare down the fence line toward the entrance gate. I turned my lawn chair in the other direction. I could see the ranch house and part of the barn behind it. I kept turning until I faced the shaded valley floor in the direction of Old Cabin. I had just made out its lines when a murder of crows flew down in front of the abandoned dwelling, quickly assessed seeds and grasses available in the area, then slithered back into the trees. Spikes of sunlight touched a few departing birds, revealing a silver snakiness in these black creatures. They had some glamour of light in them, like movie vampires.

My focus returned to Old Cabin. An old man in a wide sombrero was now standing under the cabin porch. A second figure huddled in the shadows against the wall. I sensed it was a woman. I knew immediately, although I could not see his eyes at all, that the man was staring right at me. I waved and turned away. Who were they? Ben and Valentina?

After dinner I unpacked my suitcases. Everything seemed to have a natural place with the exception of my pistol. I finally stored it in a middle drawer of the bedroom bureau underneath a pile of shirts. I had my laptop with me, and looked around for the internet access I had been promised in Ben's posted description of Shady Grove Cabin.

Supposedly the place had been wired for ethernet and WiFi. I plugged my computer into a wall outlet behind the desk in my sitting room, and tried the password Ben had given me, "valley101." Connection made. Then I read a few chapters of the new Michael Connelly thriller. Satisfying as always.

I had a nightcap on the porch. Thinking over my day, I fell into a doze. A bit later—it couldn't have been more than a few minutes—I was catapulted into full alertness by the careening highlights, screeching tires, and roaring exhaust of a vehicle headed like a bat out of hell toward the mouth of the canyon. The rabbit from Disney's *Alice in Wonderland* popped into my mind. Somebody late, so late for a very important date, probably somebody from one of the canyon's interior spreads.

I had promised myself that I would try to keep a diary during this wilderness downtime. I wrote a brief entry on the computer, then went immediately to sleep.

I dreamed that I was crawling into a tunnel or mineshaft. It kept narrowing. I felt scraping on my back, then on the top of my head, then on my chin and cheeks. The opening got tighter and tighter. I could scarcely wiggle. I kept struggling . . . until my lungs filled with sweet air. I continued on, past the worst of it. At last I felt a kind of release into perfection, as if I had come through terrible barriers to the right place.

I awoke sweating but happy. I had come through. Somehow, I had come through. Birth. The dream had to be about birth. Black Ash Canyon was my home for the time being. I had come through, and I was starting anew again.

CHAPTER THREE

It wasn't long before the day sounded its first anxious chord.

I awoke just after dawn. A glance out the bedroom window told me that fog had settled in overnight. I did my usual routine, stretching, washing, shaving. Throwing on a warm athletic jacket, I made coffee and spread butter and apricot jam on two pieces of toast.

I took my modest breakfast out to the porch. My chair was where I had left it last night, turned toward the road. Setting my toast and coffee down on a weathered redwood table, I started repositioning the chair before I realized that I did not want to look at Old Cabin. Before that thought fully jelled I had again locked eyes with the sombreroed man standing, exactly as he had the previous evening, on the porch of Old Cabin a hundred yards away. He was partially obscured by the pewter mists of morning fog. I felt changes. The woman beside him at our last encounter was no longer there. I didn't wave this time, for there was no greeting in his stare. He was clinging to me like a life raft. Who was he?

I carted my dishes inside and finished dressing. I decided that the best thing to do was to take a walk that would begin with a visit to Old Cabin. Face to face with the mystery man, I would soon learn if he really did for some reason need my help.

When I reemerged, the old man was no longer on the porch. All right. I would soon discover what was what. The closer I came to Old Cabin, the more run-down it seemed. The exterior had once been painted blue, but only occasional patches of color still showed on its warped and dusty planks. "Hello," I said, my voice raised but short of shouting. Old Cabin didn't answer. So I said it again, louder. Again there was no answer. I stepped onto the porch. The old wood creaked, buckling a bit under my weight. I knocked on the door.

"Is anyone there?"

I knocked again. Then I heard a sound inside, like a chain dropped gently on a floor, a clang followed by a silvery chime of settling links. I decided that I had discharged my obligations. I stepped off the porch and continued walking toward Outlaw Creek.

The vegetation was different on this side of the canyon. Someone in the old days—perhaps Ben's uncle Lars Griswold—had planted a stand of Monterey pines. They were enormous at this point, a hundred feet high or more. I reached the dry bed of Outlaw Creek, lined with alders and arroyo willows. Twenty yards to the east, on the crest of a rise, stood a dark green A-frame that had to be Creekside Chalet. A wispy trail of smoke escaped from its rock chimney. A new black Range Rover was parked at the foot of stairs leading to its front door. Through the nearby trees I spotted a dirt road headed toward the main compound.

Ben had told me that Solly Barlow disdained ordinary social existence, but I doubted he would mind if one of his few neighbors dropped in to say hello. Besides, after my disconcerting experience at Old Cabin, company, even the company of a crackpot hermit, was a welcome thought.

I climbed up the railed stairs and approached the front door. An old horseshoe had been mounted on a swivel bracket against a brass plate. I gave it a couple of firm taps. A dog began barking inside the cabin. At length a balding, bearded man in a red wool Pendleton shirt answered the door with a German shepherd at his side. I introduced myself, and he followed suit. "Solomon Barlow. Do come in, Mr. Buckman." I entered a high-ceilinged, pine-paneled room with a no-fuss kitchen at one end and a fireplace at the other, flanked by a small couch and two sagging wing chairs. A couple of worn Native American saddle blankets had been mounted on the wall. Barlow excused himself, and put the excited dog, whose name was Hughes, in a back room.

"I don't have many visitors," he said as we sat down. "But I've been researching you on the internet."

So much for a fresh start. "Oh."

"You're a movie scholar." He looked as if the thought amused him.

"I'm sure you found out more than that."

"You mean all those news stories about your marriage? That's just media slop. I paid it no mind. But those movie books you've done. I had to laugh about those. You may not believe this, but I've only seen around ten movies in my whole life."

He had grown up, as he put it, "wherever the new oil was," in Alaska, Venezuela, and the North Sea primarily  His parents had not been at all interested in entertainment. He wasn't either.

"Which of the movies is your favorite?" I immediately regretted the question. Here was a living American male whose mind, whose dreams and desires, were virtually untouched by the motion picture industry, and I was asking him for his Top Ten list. How pointless and corrupt was that? Still, my curious soul waited for his answer.

"Oh, they had some movies at a field my father helped to open in Alaska, and one of the senior toolpushers thought I ought to see *Tulsa.* A lively red-haired woman was in it. I liked her. Is that supposed to be a good one in your circles?"

"It has its champions. I remember a moment at the end where the film jumps ahead into the future, and the oil wells of one field become the several thousand oil wells of modern Tulsa."

He got excited. "Sonofabitch! Pardon my language, but I remember that too. That was the best part of it!"

We went off on oil drilling for a few minutes before I brought him back to the Griswold Ranch.

"I want to ask you something, Solly. Is there anybody living in Old Cabin?" I told him about the man I had seen yesterday and this morning. He looked away from me and began scratching his ankle. It was apparent that the subject made him uneasy.

"I haven't seen anybody, not personally. You should talk to the Griswolds about that."

He clearly knew something about Old Cabin, but was not about to tell me. So I made small talk for a while. I asked what he did with himself here in Black Ash Canyon. He liked feeding the birds. He and Hughes hiked in the mornings and afternoons. At night he read. He fancied Jack London, Rex Beach, Wilbur Smith. Once a week a friendly woman from the supermarket in Lassiter Springs delivered his groceries. His son Aaron, who lived in San Diego, visited now and then.

"Don't care much for modern civilization," he declared. "If I want to check in on the latest things, I use the computer. Otherwise, I get along fine, and I wish modern civilization would get along fine without me. If the do-gooders and their support team of bureaucrats just wanted my cooperation, it might be tolerable. 'Here's my tax check. Now leave me alone.' But that's not enough these days. They want to be loved. Hell, they want to be *worshipped!* So the government sends me its yearly load of forms, and always gets angry when I refuse their wonderful benefits and programs. When I tell them that I don't care to enroll, don't care to (as they put it) *take advantage of* this or that, they try to cram this or that down my throat, then expect me to say 'Thanks, man, that really *was* wonderful. You know-it-alls were right again.'"

Self-reliance, self-sufficiency, a "Don't Tread on Me" mentality: the old virtues touted by the likes of Ralph Waldo Emerson. I had never encountered so pure a case of the classic American individualism that my high-school and college textbooks so unanimously deplored.

"I think I've earned the right to take care of myself," Solly told me as his rant lost its steam. "I provided for that. I have money in the bank and a quarter share in a fine local company."

"What company is that?"

"Obispo Petroleum. Today's a Friday." He glanced at his watch. "Our trucks will be here any moment now to empty the tanks on Ben Griswold's horsehead wells."

The dog released a chain of barks from the back of the house.

"Maybe you should go now, Mr. Buckman. I have to let Hughes out. He's nervous today."

Outside the morning fog still lay heavy on the valley floor. I started walking along Outlaw Creek toward the western boundary of the Griswold Ranch. A distant figure appeared through the mist ahead of me, coming my way. I soon recognized her as Valentina Griswold. She seemed oblivious to the brisk morning air, and wore the same sun dress she had on yesterday for her graveyard ride.

I moved through rough land, on the lookout for boulders and declivities. She approached at an even pace, seeming to float through the glowing air. I put the difference down to her superior knowledge of the terrain.

"Good morning, Mrs. Griswold."

She stopped, looked me over. "Mr. Buckman. Aren't you going to ask me what I'm looking for?"

I decided to humor her. It was perhaps a good sign that she recognized me and knew my name. "All right, then. What *are* you looking for?"

She smiled. "A sharp knife to cut off your head with."

That gave me a chill, as she must have intended. The poor woman's mind was again blundering along in chaos and incoherence. "Can I see you home?"

"You should know better than that, Mr. Buckman. No one is home around here. This isn't the world. You should examine the maps."

I was formulating a question about those maps when I noticed a crude tattoo on her naked forearm. Not a real tattoo, but drawn, perhaps with felt-tip pens. It pictured a knife. The knife seemed oddly short to me, not longer than an inch, until I realized that the blade was meant to be buried in her arm almost to the hilt. Three curving drops of red blood fell like tears from the mouth of the wound.

"Do let me take you home. It's not far."

Suddenly she was jolly. "No, it's *not* far, and I'll be fine. You must finish your walk on such a lovely morning. Maybe you would rather walk with Shy?"

I hesitated. Then I looked again at her homemade tattoo. "No, I think we should walk back together."

Suddenly she was concerned. "I'm not the poor afflicted soul here, Michael. *You are.* You look as if you've seen a ghost. But no. It's just your father's coat hanging up." She stepped forward and kissed my cheek. "I'll be on my way now."

Before I could decide what to do she was off at a smart clip. I turned and saw her leave the creek bed, angling off into the woods. I thought over her words, trying to fix them in my memory. She had not, of course, made conventional sense, but there was an eerie penetration, a strange matter-of-factness to her disjointed ramblings. A knife to cut off my head with. This isn't the world. Check the maps. No ghost, but my father's clothes hanging up. I didn't see how these could be personal communications meant for me in the usual way, though one of her oracles had sent my thoughts winging back to my own childhood. Had she been recalling a book? Some configuration of past events?

I walked on down the bank of Outlaw Creek. Now I could see that I was indeed on a well-worn path. I walked about a mile into the canyon, and saw one of Ben's oil wells nodding away through the trees. A bit further on, the creek turned to the left just as a narrow, twisting arroyo cut into the main canyon.

I stopped, shivering. Winds must funnel down this side canyon, I thought, zipping my jacket more tightly about my neck. I crossed the creek bed and climbed a ways to get a better look up the draw. The fog had begun to clear from the sky. Two hawks soared lazily in and out of the mist. There seemed to be evidence of an old road, but now grown over with brush. At the bottom of the gulch was a rocky area with patches of smoothed soil. I guessed that a tiny rivulet of water from this arroyo fed Outlaw Creek during the rainy season. That season wasn't far off according to the forecast on my computer homepage last night. Rain was expected early next week.

As I started to walk back over the stream bed, I noticed a group of rocks arranged in an unnatural shapeliness. They formed a circle about five feet in diameter. Intersecting at the center were two perpendicular lines of rocks. The whole structure looked like the cross hairs of a gun sight pointing straight to the entrance of the side canyon. But the place at the very center, where the hairs would have crossed, was not occupied by a stone. There was an old rusty hoop there, wider than an inch, but not much wider, and seemingly balanced on the ground.

I got down on my knees, hooked my forefinger in the iron hoop, and pulled. No give at all. So I got two fingers into the hoop and pulled harder. This time a long iron spike emerged from the ground, just over a foot long in my estimate. It was formed of a sharp iron rod welded to an iron loop. It seemed old. What was it for? I thought it looked like a skewer used in cooking.

A strong impulse came over me to put the spike back in the ground and leave this spot. Maybe it was just the idea that I was a stranger here and had disturbed an arrangement that had taken someone considerable trouble to achieve. I gave in, shoving the spike back into the center of the rock design and packing earth around it.

I started back. When I caught sight of the Creekside Chalet, I heard a commotion through the trees. Ben was shouting. I jogged through the large pines, then a stand of sycamores, and burst into the clearing above the ranch house. The front porch and side wall of Old Cabin were in flames. Ben was streaming water on the blaze from a thick hose connected to a tank beside his garage. He was shouting to Cheyenne, who had just run out of the garage carrying a pick and shovel. I intersected her, putting out my hands. She gave me the tools and ran back toward the garage.

"Ben, tell me what to do!"

He turned my way. "Thank God you're here. Shovel as much dirt as you can on the porch and the back walls!"

The ground was hard. I broke it up with repeated strokes of the pick, then shoveled heaps of dirt and clods onto the porch. The porch roof collapsed on one side, so I concentrated on throwing dirt in the middle area. Flung from my shovel, it smacked repeatedly against the door. A wild thought took me back to my polite knocks of two hours ago. How much ruder and more urgent I was now! Soon Cheyenne was at my side with another pick and shovel.

There was a window, opaque with dirt, between the fallen section of the porch roof and the front door. I recalled, or hoped I recalled, that fires were best ventilated, so I grabbed a rock dislodged by my pick and threw it through the window. There was a sound like rushing water, followed by a column of leaping flame. "Ben!" I yelled. "Over here!"

He came around and shot calming water through the open window. Soon it looked to be over. Ben stepped gingerly toward the window and looked around. "I can't see any flames," he told us. He kept spraying for a while, and we kept throwing dirt. At almost the same time we all stopped work. The place stank of smoke and charred wood. The front porch was damaged beyond repair. Yet the structure still stood. It had taken a huge punch, but had not gone down.

Cheyenne began to cry. Ben put his arms around her. "Shush now," he said. "The old place weathered the storm. We've seen worse than this. Leave Tina to me. I'll tell her about this. Maybe she won't be as heartbroken as you think."

I wondered if she would be heartbroken at all. Anyone looking for evidence that this was not the world, but some kind of after-life of the world, might find a pleasure of confirmation in the new face of Old Cabin.

Ben walked back to the ranch house to tell Valentina about the fire. Cheyenne and I returned our picks and shovels to the tool rack on the garage wall. She thanked me for pitching in. "I hope Ben is right about mother. Old Cabin contains a lot of memories for her. She was born in it, you know."

"Back when Angel and Consuela lived there."

She didn't conceal her pleasure at my knowingness. "Daddy must have given you quite a history lesson."

"We both enjoyed the talk."

"Listen, Mr. Buckman. Mike. It is 'Mike,' isn't it, not Michael?"

"When my parents liked me it was 'Mike.' When I was a bad boy, and they wanted to teach me a lesson, it was always 'Michael.'"

"Mike, then. Shall we go into town for dinner tonight? I was going to ask you before my favorite building on the whole ranch caught on fire, but I really want to ask you now. There's a nice place in Las Sombras, not touristy, not yuppie. My friends and I have been going there for years—the Stagecoach Bar & Grill. Not fancy either, but nice and welcoming. What do you say?"

"What would your father say? He asked me if I was going to be a good tenant, and I said yes. I wouldn't want to disappoint him."

"Look, I know that Time has yet to put his unimaginable touch on me." Her eyeballs shot heavenward, then back down to me. "But I'm thirty years old, and well able to make my own choices. Besides, I'm not throwing myself at you, I'm asking you to dinner. There are things we have to talk about."

"I'm sure there must be. Things on my side too."

"It's a date?"

"It's a date. Shall I drive?"

"Yes. I'll be over at the Shady Grove and ready to go at 7:00, come hell or high water. I guess we've already had hell."

So. There was to be another side to this weird and baffling day. A surprise romantic intrigue. A cowgirl who could quote in idle banter Wordsworth's "unimaginable touch of Time." I recalled uneasily that it was the braininess of Carolyn Nast that had first attracted me at that presentation on Douglas Fairbanks. If I was going anywhere with this girl, I was going slowly.

I went back to my cabin, showered, and made myself a snack. I opened my laptop with the thought of getting a head start on today's diary entry when I heard a car drive into the ranch. I got up and looked out the window. It was a County Sheriff's vehicle. The siren was off, but the blue lights on top were flashing. It pulled up in front of the Griswold home. I turned away. This had to be related to the fire.

Wrong. The dour tone poem of the day had just introduced a surprising new theme.

Twenty minutes later the sheriff's car drove up to Shady Grove Cabin, and an officer knocked on my door. He introduced himself as Terry Coleman.

"Sorry to bother you. I gather this is your first day living in Black Ash Canyon. But this morning we found a dead woman—strike that—a *murdered* woman just up the way at one of Ben Griswold's oil wells. The tank truck driver, doing his usual Friday run, found her about an hour ago. Not much of an effort was made to hide her. She was, well, slashed up pretty bad. *Brutally,* in fact. We don't have an ID yet, but she was young, blond, and might have been pretty. The coroner's quick estimate is that she was killed around twelve to fifteen hours ago."

I took it in as best I could. "So you're wondering if I saw or heard anything that might bear on the crime?"

"That's it. Nice and simple."

"Maybe I did." I told him about having a nightcap on the porch last night, and seeing the headlights of a speeding vehicle streak down the road toward Las Sombras.

"Do you know the time?"

"Not exactly. After midnight but not later than one would be my best guess."

Coleman asked me a lot of questions bearing on the type of vehicle I had seen. The thing was, I hadn't really *seen* the vehicle, just its headlights.

"But," he reminded me, "you can often see the outline of a vehicle, or at least its grill and hood, from the glow of the headlights, or see the outline of the trunk from its taillight glow."

I was sure it was not a truck—not a transport rig, not even a pickup. It was lower, more agile. Possibly a passenger car. Possibly a small SUV, but not a large one or a van. I spoke of my walk in the woods this morning. But I saw no reason to make unnecessary trouble for the Griswold family, so I left out Valentina's crazy remark about cutting my head off and the hand-drawn knife tattoo on her arm. Surely she had nothing to do with the vicious murder of a stranger.

When I had run out of information, Coleman thanked me, handed me a card, and drove off.

Ben Griswold had told me the canyon was a big tinder-box. I had already seen a fire. Tina Griswold had told me the canyon was not the world, that no one was at home here. I had already seen a horror movie's worth of eeriness. Now I had a woman cut to ribbons *brutally* at an old donkey well on a remote stretch of my new backyard. This sounded serious, this sounded big publicity, this sounded serial killer. At the very least my desire for anonymity, peace and quiet, and all kindred hopes and dreams had just been blown to smithereens.

The morning fire might have burned some modern squatters out of Old Cabin. But I too, in my way, had just been burned into homelessness. I had arrived in this apparent wilderness twenty-four hours ago. I could not help but glance ahead. What else might be waiting in the thick shadows of Black Ash Canyon?

# CHAPTER FOUR

Cheyenne knocked on the door of Shady Grove Cottage as darkness was falling. She was dressed in white chinos and a loose white cotton blouse. Had there been the blouse only, her figure would have been shrouded in mystery. But a fitted red vest with black and gold brocade outlined her natural proportions. I was grateful for that. Shy was an attractive gal, no doubt about it. A glistening lipstick matched the vest. She looked like she smelled good.

"Do you like the art?" she asked me.

"I noticed it was different from the pictures on the internet. Is that your doing?"

It surely was. She had majored in art history at UC Santa Barbara. Her first job out of college was in an interesting store in Montecito. One side held beautifully printed art books, the other a gallery of modern art. She managed the books. Two years ago, her mother's health failing, she had returned to the ranch to help out her parents.

"I love the Hockney poster in the bedroom. Pleasant to look at one of his sparkling swimming pools before and after sleep. That Sutherland study of Churchill over the desk was a bit daunting at first. Sir Winston destroyed the finished painting, didn't he?"

"Yes. His wife said it made him look disenchanted. Sutherland said he was trying to capture the rocklike quality of the great man's face."

"It is, yes, rocklike, but you can stare through that to his spirit." I love to chat about art, but just then my thoughts were racing in other directions. "Listen, I've been wanting to talk to someone, to *you*, about what's going on around here." I recounted my experiences with the figures on the Old Cabin front porch, the odd stone design in the bed of Outlaw Creek, my meeting with her mother.

Something in my last encounter with Valentina had tripped memories of my childhood. She insisted that I pose a question to her. "Aren't you going to ask me what I am looking for?" When, playing along, I did ask, her answer was "A knife to cut your head off with." The exchange seemed akin to childhood jokes and games of the "guess what I am thinking" variety, like Twenty Questions, which my family had always played on car trips. These sorts of amusement always began with a formula. "I am thinking of . . ." or "Knock knock." Things never got off the ground unless another player, in response to the initial trigger, said "Is it animal, vegetable, or mineral?" or "Who's there?"

Suspecting that Valentina's fragmented, distressed mind was playing an old game, I had spent some computer time that afternoon trying to locate the exact one. Eventually I downloaded a nineteenth-century book on American children's games, and there it was. The author called it "The Madrid Game" because the earliest example he knew was played there around 1840. A short form of Madrid began with "Sister, what are you looking for?" The knife to kill you with was the immediate answer. A longer version began with "Mother, what are you looking for?" and took a more roundabout and suspenseful way to the destined end. A needle. What do you need a needle for? To sew my bag. Why do you need a bag? To put my steel in. Why do you need a steel? To sharpen the knife to cut your head off with.

"Interesting game, eh? Don't answer that by asking why! But here's a child bursting with curious questions for a forthcoming sister or mother until she learns of her relative's murderous intent. It's like a template for a really good detective story, one about a little girl detective whose inquiries provoke or expose a desire to murder her."

Cheyenne had been nodding her head. Now she took a deep breath and began talking.

"I remember playing that game with my mother. She had played it with her mother. We used to laugh about how awful the game was, though we knew at the same time that it gave us strange pleasure. I'm afraid this is typical of mother's mental state in recent years. It's like she's desperate for familiar things, and runs back to old games and songs from her childhood, the first books she read, the first tall tales she heard.

"Mike, I think I should start with Old Cabin." She searched my face. "But this is embarrassing."

I shrugged. "Believe you me, I know embarrassing. You can be as embarrassing as you want around me. I'm not judgmental." I broke into my most winning smile. "Honest. Try me."

She smiled back. "OK. Let's see if you mean it. There *are* ghosts, or there were until recently, in Old Cabin."

The ghost couple weren't there all the time. But they had always been a presence in her life. Sometimes at dusk Shy would look toward the Old Cabin porch, and the two of them, the man in a sombrero and his female companion, would just be standing there, as much a feature of the world as she was, as appreciative of the beauty of the moment. Shy would head off some place, and notice them on the way out from the ranch, standing sentinel or performing some . . . well, *official task*. Their job, she had always assumed, was to smile on the Griswold Ranch, to bring cheer and continuity to the people who lived and worked there. They were ancestors. They were the ghosts of Angel and Consuela

Acosta, Shy's grandparents, her mom's mom and dad. They had led their lives in that cabin, and now they were leading their deaths there.

Personally, I didn't know what to think. This looked to be a grand tale, full of choice supernatural fantasies, but I was pretty much a sceptic. To be sure, eerie experiences had of late jolted my incredulity. And the figure I had seen on the porch was looking to me for help—of that I was certain.

"If there are tragic hauntings, then I suppose there must be happy hauntings," I said, being as noncommittal as I could manage. In my mind I laid great stress on the *if.*

She was particularly taken with the fact that, before the fire, when I saw the man in the sombrero this morning, I had the distinct feeling that the woman was not with him. For she had never seen either of the ghosts alone. The had always appeared as a couple. Cheyenne feared that their departure would lead to a fuller and quicker destruction of her mother's mind. At the beginning of Tina's downward spiral she and her father had worried about incipient Alzheimer's. Then they had worried about deepening dementia and mysterious fugue states. Now, with the loss of her guardian grandparents, she feared her mother might become permanently comatose or even die. Her days of near normal functioning had become rarer and rarer. Like a little girl beginning school, she spent hours and hours in her bedroom poring over old maps. Her father had acquired, at Tina's direction, a small library of map books and atlases. She mostly stared at maps of California, but not necessarily of places she had visited or had any apparent connection to. Amid all these precise renderings of California locale, Valentina was usually lost and speechless.

It seemed to me that finishing this conversation took precedence over the nearby honky tonk.

"Would you like a drink? I've got beer. I've got Chivas Regal and bottled water."

"Beer."

"I've also got some of those blue corn chips. They're salty enough to be good."

"Sold."

I brought out refreshments.

The couple in Old Cabin had never caused her social discomfort. Some of her friends did not seem to notice the pair. Others would claim to see them, then stop seeing them until their memories of having once done so faded into apparent dreams or fantasies. Theo Steele's boy, Billy, was a partial exception.

Her father suspected the worst of the entire Steele family, and disapproved of Cheyenne playing with little Billy. But

Billy was close by, about her age, and had a lively mind. He thought too highly of himself, no doubt about that. Valentina used to say that the boy was always tooting his own horn. His shameless bragging got still worse after he graduated from Cal Poly with a degree in civil engineering.

But Billy was a smart smartass. Though he never saw the ghostly couple, he believed that the Griswold family did. He felt lucky to be close to such rare happenings. "I've been looking in the school library," he told Shy when they were ten years old, "and most ghosts aren't at all like yours. They are angry, they want to get back at someone. They aim to hurt us." A few years later, Billy Steel's interest in the spirits of the Griswold Ranch had become pre-professional. He wanted to go over every inch of Old Cabin with a boy's supernatural investigator kit of compass, thermometer, magnet, pendulum, and night goggles. He was just as eager to explore other "interesting places" on the Griswold property.

At this point Ben Griswold did what he had always threatened to do, and banished the boy from his ranch. Ben loved his ghosts. He feared that Billy, with his brash intrusive ways, his youthful intellectual arrogance, would drive away the guardian spirits.

That didn't stop the impulsive and resourceful Mr. Steele from writing and calling and seeing Cheyenne at school and school functions. Ben would not allow her to date him, even if she had wanted that. But Billy always felt that the two of them were destined for each other. They would outlive their warring parents, combine the Griswold Ranch with the Steele Ranch, and shine the light of modern ghost research into all the "hot spots" on the Steele-Griswold Ranch.

Cheyenne did the eyes heavenward routine at this point in her story, indicating that she definitely had no romantic interest in Billy. He had been a fun playmate. Today he was swell for reminiscing and sharing a few laughs. She had explained her feelings often enough that Billy in his maturity had developed a high degree of independence, apparently accepting the fact that his early dreams were not going to come true. He was married for a while. But there were clear indications that Billy Steele was in some ways still under the sway of those first boyhood dreams. In high school he formed a club known as the Haunt Squad. They traveled to supposedly ghost-ridden houses, beaches, swamps, mountains, and camped out there, seeking first-hand experiences of paranormal phenomena. They looked through California newspapers for stories with an occult angle, then tracked them down. After college he tried to build a business on this foundation. He rented a store front in Las Sombras and hung a neon sign in the window announcing the commercial headquarters of Ghost Killers.

Ah. Now I knew what the neon sign was doing on a pre-fab metal building in remote Black Ash Canyon.

"Good name, don't you think?" Shy asked me, her eyes dancing.

"A good name can take you a long ways," I replied. "I mean, think of the Sex Pistols!"

She laughed. "Good one. Of course, even a bad name can succeed. Think of The Beatles! Billy, though, good name and all, didn't make it."

I saw a nice long vein of mutual private humor open up, and I wanted to communicate my interest in working it together. So I continued in that vein. "Along the lines of the Beatles, you have to consider Led Zeppelin. That's a real bad name, right next door to Lead Balloon."

We soon got back to Billy Steele's business career. The idea was that clients experiencing disturbing hauntings would come to Ghost Killers in the same way that people with ants and rats went to an exterminator. An experienced team of ghost exterminators would investigate the hauntings and submit recommendations along with detailed cost estimates. Billy knew that many paranormal investigators worked for little or nothing, but he thought they were in most cases plodding frauds, and assumed that the well-off residents of Las Sombras would prefer his aggressive, college-educated approach.

But business never rose above a faint trickle. Catholics with ghost problems always consulted the priest in San Bernardino who was known to perform private exorcisms and house-cleansings with crosses, incense, and Holy Water. The scientifically minded preferred a team from Los Angeles armed with the latest and most expensive gear. Celebrities wanted their ghost issues to be addressed by a group in San Diego that had their own cable ghost-hunting show. There simply weren't enough clients left over to float Billy Steele's Ghost Killers. He wrote a couple of books on his theories about spirits from beyond and how to evict them. One was published by a Santa Cruz press specializing in paranormal subjects. Another, more a pamphlet than a book, he paid to have privately printed. Finally Billy called it quits on the business front, and retired to the Steele Ranch where, much to the relief of his father Theo, he began repairing tractors and harvesters for local farmers.

"I suppose I'm destined to meet this Billy Steele character."

"I'm afraid so. It's written in the stars. He'll be calling me tonight, and when he doesn't get me, he'll start in again tomorrow morning. He'll want to meet with me— especially now that they found a dead body by our oil well. And with you also, Mike, since you have direct knowledge of the recent happenings at Old Cabin."

"I also want to ask you about the murder."

"I understand. But could we table that subject for tonight?"

I nodded assent.

"Are you getting hungry?"

I started picking up our empties, humming Willie Nelson's *On the Road Again.*


On the road again, I drove my truck in utter darkness through the brief stretch of Black Ash Canyon Pass between the Griswold spread and Las Sombras. When I passed the graveyard where I had first seen Tina Griswold, I asked Shy about it. The cemetery had once been the unofficial resting ground of the town of Las Sombras, but as the area became more prosperous, residents found the old and relatively sunless plot in the narrow canyon mouth rather forbidding, and chose to enjoy eternal rest in a new sunnier cemetery built on the flat ground to the north of town. These days only inhabitants of the canyon wound up in the shadowy old graveyard.

Shy directed me to the Stagecoach Bar & Grill, which was on one of the main cross streets in Las Sombras, but down the way a bit, near the outskirts of town. There were lots of trucks in the dirt parking lot. I had wanted to blend in around here. The white Ram had been a good choice for that. The vehicle had already picked up a veneer of fine dust from the canyon winds. It fit right in at the Stagecoach, as it had at the supermarket in Lassiter Springs.

A banner near the door trumpeted that a group called Arrowhead was playing tonight. Shy seemed acquainted with the head server, which was a good thing, for she found us a table within a few minutes. The other people in the cue gave us nasty looks as she seated us in a choice location at the far end of the dance floor, close to the bar.

We ate. A burger and yam fries for me, ribs and cole slaw for her. We danced. Arrowhead, fronted by two lead vocalists, male and female, covered old rock songs like *Sea Cruise* and *House of Blue Lights*, along with country numbers such as *Truck Drivin' Man* and *You Win Again*, and led us to invent a dance response with a base of swing jive, a touch of the frug and a pinch of square dancing, changing partners with like-minded couples. There was, blessedly, the occasional country weeper or love ballad, to which we danced close and slow, getting to know each other. She did smell good.

In between dances Shy's friends would approach our table and sit down for a spell. A guy named Jeremiah, known to all as Just Plain Jerry, told funny stories involving Shy at the Sadie Hawkins Dance and the Senior Prom at Las Sombras High. Another fellow, whom Shy knew from her art studies at UC Santa Barbara, sat with us for an hour. He was apprenticed to a local sculptor, and told us how excited he was to be liberating a lion cub from an extraordinary block of orange-veined white marble from Italy. Leanne, an old field hockey teammate from UC Santa Barbara, told a long story about Shy getting a bloody knee early in the game, then demanding to go back in and eventually scoring the winning goal. Betsy, a freckled red-head, told of a night at the now-defunct Mountain View Drive-In when Shy had puked in the lap of her eager boyfriend, who had failed to recognize clear indications of stomach distress.

We were both growing weary when Lorna Gonsalves appeared at our table. She came on right away as a dynamo of gab, capable of moving both sides of an imaginary conversation. Lorna worked for one of those zombie newspapers, *The*

*Las Sombras Sun*, that gave away copies for nothing because they were supported by their advertisers. It carried local columns and stories, movie and food reviews, profiles of notable residents, and pages and pages of advertising. She was at present just the new restaurant reviewer, but she had news.

"I haven't seen you in here lately, Shy. It made me wonder if your mother is OK? I bet she'll get better soon. You know, when she is better, I would love to interview her for the *Sun*. I bet she has some great stories about the old days. Aren't you going to introduce me to your new cowboy? He doesn't look like he's from around here."

Shy introduced us, mentioning that I was a new tenant on the Griswold Ranch. I told Lorna I was from the Paso Robles area.

"That's close enough! We'll treat you like a native son. Are there lots of boys from Paso as tall and blue-eyed and dark as you? You *have* been busy, Shy. And that murdered girl found on your ranch. Imagine, *that's* starting up again! Maybe the State Police will send in a profiler right away this time. They have to have a specialist or two in copycat killers. Probably two or three *units* with that specialty. It really took a lot of balls for this new guy to dump a kill at The Fountain of Sorrow. They identified the victim, you know. Vera

Maarten, her parents ran a restaurant in New Aarhus. Ever been to The Viking Nook on Hans Christian Andersen Boulevard? That's their place. The copycat used a knife on her, you know, right off the bat."

Cheyenne had several times glanced at me uncertainly during this gushy discharge of pseudo-friendly venom.

"That's quite enough, Lorna."

"Why. . . ." She looked at Shy, then at me, then back at Shy, her expression turning to one of dumbfounded open-mouthed shock. "You haven't told him, have you? He doesn't know anything about Dieter, the Black Ash Canyon murders, the notebooks! Don't you think he has, I dunno, a *right* to know? He is paying to live with you, isn't he? I would think it only Christian to tell him in no uncertain terms just what he has gotten himself into!"

Shy was furious. "Damn you Lorna, I've had it up to here with your phony advice and your phony friendship!" I'm sure this was intended as a mere prelude to a truly serious chewing-out, but I never found out for certain, because the lights in the bar suddenly went out save for a couple of blue spots.

"It's the last Friday of the month at the Stagecoach, and it's midnight, or will be in, let's see, thirty seconds," Arrowhead's male lead announced, pointing to the antique Ford

Motor Company clock over the bar. Its big second hand had just rounded the clock's Antarctica and was heading up to the North Pole of midnight.

Lorna, wide-eyed, nodded at Cheyenne. "Your friend from Paso is going to see it all now. You should never have tried to keep him in the dark, Cheyenne Griswold. Look over in the back corner." She gestured in that direction. "Annette Pruitt is here."

The singer snapped his fingers a couple of times. "You all know what time it is?" he asked the room. Then, answering his question, Arrowhead broke into the opening lines of a classic Buck Owens tune.

*Oh it's cryin' time again, you're gonna leave me. I can see that faraway look in your eyes. . . .*

Stagecoach patrons seemed to be holding a collective breath, waiting for the dam to break. The sound of forlorn tears rose from that back table to which Lorna had gestured. Here and there other women joined in. The music was rich and bluesy. Guitars gently wept. It was truly, in this bar, cryin' time again. The song as written was about being left by a beloved. At this country hotspot in Las Sombras, the old song had become a mourning chant. You could tell from the style of the crying. These women weren't just jilted. They were bereft. Their loved ones were dead. Those eyes had a really *faraway look.*

On the road again, I broke the awkward silence. "Look, I know this subject was tabled for the evening. But you might as well tell me now. *What was all of that about?* Who is Annette Pruitt? Who is this Black Ash Canyon Killer?"

I heard a sigh. I thought she might be crying.

"I knew all of this was coming. I just wanted to hold it off for a night. We were having a good time, weren't we?"

"Of course we were. We still are."

"All right, then. Twenty years ago we had a serial killer in these parts. He dumped all three of his victims in Black Ash Canyon. Reporters dubbed him the Black Ash Canyon Killer. His first was Mary Pruitt, and her body was found at one of our oil wells. Dad started calling it the "Fountain of Sorrow." That's where they found Vera Maarten's body this morning. The killer turned out to be a young man from New Aarhus, Dieter Thorson."

"So this new killer does have every earmark of being a copycat?"

"A super copycat, maybe, an advanced copycat."

"I'm not sure I follow you."

"Look, Mike, I don't want to say another word about this situation until tomorrow. Once Billy Steele gets into this, everything will change. He's very forceful. I'm sure my phone will be ringing when I get home. I'm sure Billy will set up a meeting for tomorrow. You've seen what happened to our local honky tonk. They have been doing that song at midnight on the last Friday of the month for twenty years now, ever since Vera Pruitt was killed on the Wednesday night before that Friday. That's a lot of tears. Her sister Annette has probably shed more of them than anyone else. But Dieter Thorson's other victims also had people to cry for them. And now we have a new victim to recharge the tradition. And my mother. God, Mike, what will happen to her now that her parents are gone? I think her sorrow is already too deep for tears."

I reached over to take her hand, but withdrew when she began to speak again. "To tell you the truth, I hate that ritual. I saw the connection to Dieter Thorson when the police came by. So did they. But I forgot that the timing of this new murder matched his. Had I noticed that this was the last Friday in September, I would never have gone to the Stagecoach. I really do hate it. Why our ranch? Why does every fucking woman-killer around here drop bodies on our ranch? I hate being forced to become a human jackpump, made to throw out tears as regularly as our wells spew out oil. The sorrow just *takes over.*" And then she was crying.

We had just come onto the snaky turns and switchbacks of Black Ash Canyon Pass. I stopped the car, leaving the lights on and everything running. I put my arms around her and held her until she ran out of tears.

"'Fountain of Sorrow?' Ben changed the name of the well after it became killing ground for this Dieter Thorson?"

"That's right. He even joked that the well had always been a sorrow, since it only produced a few barrels a day."

"Are we talking about one of the wells that used to belong to the Steele Ranch?"

"Daddy obviously gave you a complete run-down."

"Well, I would say that 'Fountain of Sorrow' is another good name. Your father has a sense of poetry. Your mother does too. *Quite* a sense of poetry in her case."

"Can you stand my screwed-up family? Really, I wouldn't think any the less of you if you simply packed up and went somewhere else."

"I don't have to stand your screwed-up family. I went to dinner with you, not them."

"But I brought them along, didn't I?"

"Come on, now. The whole damn town brought them along. History brought them along. Stop accusing yourself."

I had just noticed in the glow of my headlights that I had pulled up next to the old cemetery. I started driving again.

I let Shy off at the ranch house. There wasn't much left to say to each other. I hugged her again and kissed her briefly.

Home, I cleaned up my kitchen, thinking of Cheyenne Griswold. She needed help. Her family needed help. I had come here to help myself, and I needed it too. But my need was not as acute as hers. I thought about the ghosts (really?) and the serial killers (really!) surrounding her. A nice mess I had gotten myself into! But I would not leave the canyon, not yet.

I wasn't here because I was unspeakably in love with the girl, like the romantic Chaplin. I wasn't here because I was magically oblivious to the danger, like the deadpan Keaton. I did feel an odd confidence that, whatever lay ahead, it was somehow within my spectrum of possibilities. And that, for now, was good enough. Full steam ahead.

CHAPTER FIVE

We had a one o'clock appointment with Billy Steele. So early Saturday afternoon I drove Cheyenne to the large metal structure on the southwestern edge of the Steele Ranch. Turning off onto their access road I felt the difference between this land and the Griswold place. Here, the widened valley and lower altitude of the bordering mountains provided a normal sense of sunlight and open space. I loved my cottage under the trees in the cleft between mountains, but its setting did obscure the yawning expanse between earth and sky, us and the heavens. Humans have always preferred to live with the universe above them.

The first time I had seen the neon Ghost Killers sign it had been inexplicable. Now it seemed comforting. Whatever was going on around here, there was at least one place in Black Ash Canyon prepared to fight it. And we were there.

The entire front area of the building, Shy informed me, was a machine shop spacious enough to house major farming vehicles. Behind this shop was the large room Billy designated his "clubhouse." The space had evolved through the years, but he and his various groups of Ghost Killers had always congregated there.

A handwritten note was taped to the clubhouse door:

Hello Sly and Michael Buckman! I'm down the road on a house call and could be a few minutes late. Go on into the clubhouse, look around, have a soda, whatever. No ghosts here, and that's a personal guarantee. Will be back soon.

B. Steele (no relation to Danielle)

Shy marched in ahead of me and flipped the light switch. Large banks of fluorescent tubes, suspended from the high ceiling, hummed on. It was indeed a large room, maybe 20 feet deep and 50 feet wide, pierced by three windows in the back wall, reminding me at once of a high school auditorium, an old explorer's club, and something found below Wayne Manor. In the center was a gigantic area rug, sky blue with a pattern of what looked to be white clouds, until you realized that the clouds were all in the shape of an old airplane, perhaps a Tiger Moth. This whole area of the floor looked like a dogfight from some surreal, half-imagined war. A couple of salmon couches faced each other in the center of the carpet, with five or six brown leather club chairs set around them.

Against a side wall stood two wooden gun cases with glass doors, full of rifles and pistols, and a bank of locked metal cabinets. Next to them was a massive roll top desk. In the corner beyond was an old-style library table with overflowing piles of books and DVDs. On the opposite wall a couple of doors led to smaller rooms. One was probably a bathroom. The other might have been a roomy storage closet, or perhaps a small bedroom. The long wall opposite the entrance was taken up with bookcases, stereo equipment, a Sony flat screen, a little kitchen nook behind a small redwood picnic table with seating for six, and an upright Coke machine.

Shy got a soft-drink can from the Coke dispenser, found a magazine, and sat down on one of Billy's sofas while I began a walking tour of the clubhouse's wondrous walls. One area was decorated with early photos of the surrounding towns and several even earlier photos of a sprawling adobe ranch house. I remembered that Billy had Lassiter blood, and assumed that the adobe, with thousands upon thousands of surrounding acres, belonged to his imposing ancestor Amos Lassiter. An adjacent group of photos depicted at least three generations of Steele males posed in front of airplanes and dressed to fly them. I supposed the surreal rug in the clubhouse was Billy's tribute to their collective valor. Fearless romantic aviators stood behind him: their ceiling was his floor.

I passed on to a section of enlarged and framed book illustrations. I recognized Scrooge brought to his knees by the Ghost of Christmas Future's revelation of his own tombstone.

I thought another might depict the demonic merrymakers whirling around the maypole in Hawthorne's "Young Goodman Brown." There were others in the literary section that I could not immediately identify.

I did better with the movie posters. They included a couple of my favorites, *The Uninvited* and *Dead of Night.* A *Ghostbusters* poster showed Dan Aykroyd wielding one of those yellow-and-black ghost traps, among the most effective props in movie history. I had loved the film as a child, and couldn't prevent its demonically catchy title song from playing in my mind as I stood before the poster. We often speak of ourselves as being "haunted" by memories and songs. I had been saying that for years without paying it any mind. Now I marked *haunting memories* and *haunting tunes* for careful consideration at a later date.

Another section displayed memorabilia from Billy's time as a businessman in Las Sombras—newspaper stories, posters, programs from the local Rotary Club, the cover of *Central Coast Digest* whose lead story that month was "Ghost Killers Opens Shop in the Santa Ynez Valley." There was a photo of the storefront itself, sandwiched between two wine tasting bars, with the same neon sign that now blazed on the exterior of this vast playroom of prefabricated steel.

My tour ended at the library table. There I located the two Billy Steele publications Cheyenne had mentioned. The book, issued by the Specter Press in Santa Barbara, was entitled *The No-Nonsense Guide to Ghost Hunting*. Most of it seemed to be a polemic against the overelaborate ghost hunting equipment favored by modern paranormalists. *Death the Second Time Around: An Atheist's View of Ghost Extermination* was a fifty-page pamphlet. I had just begun skimming it when a vehicle crunched to a halt at the back of the building.

The door opened. In walked a stocky guy, his short hair prematurely gray, wearing jeans and a blue-tinted black leather jacket with a buttoned panel on its front. A circular patch, depicting the profile of a hawk's head against a yellow background, was sewn into the center of the jacket's front panel. It was clearly a replica of the Blackhawk Squadron uniform worn by the characters in an old World War II comic book.

My blood was hot. Where did he get it? I wanted one! The fantastically turned-out glamour boys of Hollywood had never shown me anything this caliber of cool. I remembered finding in a rambling junk store in Cayucos, at the age of thirteen or fourteen, Howard Chaykin's three-issue revival of the Blackhawk Squadron. Few comic books had given me more pleasure than the Chaykin *Blackhawk*.

Steele unbuttoned his jacket and threw it onto one of the chairs. Beneath it he wore a simple black sweatshirt. He exchanged greetings with Cheyenne. They hugged each other. As I walked up to them, he turned to me.

"Mike Buckman, I expect? I'm Billy Steele. Sorry I'm late. I had to fix Farmer Scott's busted harvester."

We shook hands. After some chit-chat, Billy told us to have a seat. Cheyenne and I chose opposite ends of the same salmon couch. Billy sat in the center of the couch across from us.

He began speaking to Cheyenne. "We've got two emergency situations in the canyon, both of them related to your family's ranch, Shy. As you know, I never saw the ghosts of your grandparents in Old Cabin—The Dead Zone, as you named it back then. But I assumed they were there. That was the idea I got from you and your family, and you guys would know, wouldn't you? We weren't allowed to play there, your parents made that clear. That's probably one reason we were drawn to it. Remember us putting our ears against the walls, getting excited when we heard a creak or a groan? Remember how we used to dare each other to go to sleep on that shaky front porch? I've always wanted to investigate the place. It reeks of supernatural energies. Now there's been a fire, and the ghosts are apparently gone. At the same time, a symbol of some kind, a circle with two perpendicular diameters, has appeared in the creek bed. That seems related to the Old Cabin fire."

He turned to me. "You found it, didn't you, Mike? Right at the mouth of Quicksilver Canyon?"

"If that's the name of the arroyo that opens at a bend in Outlaw Creek, yeah, I found the symbol there on Friday morning just before the fire started."

"Shy said that you first saw the spirits of Old Cabin the evening before. Tell me about that, and then about Friday morning."

I did. He kept wanting more detail, and I supplied as much as I could remember. When I was finished, he asked me if I had any written records concerning these events.

"I've been keeping a diary. I didn't write anything on Friday night, but the night before I put down something about the man in the wide straw hat."

"I'd like to see that some time."

He seemed to mean it. Myself, I failed to see the point, though satisfying his curiosity was no problem.

"I haven't noticed a computer in this room, but I suspect you have one. I could get into my computer and send the diary entry to you right now."

"It's in my desk." We went over to the ancient roll top, which, he told me, had belonged to his maternal grandfather, Jed Lassiter, who managed the general store in Lassiter Springs. Inside was a new Mac and an HP laser printer. Before long my email was in his machine with the diary file attached. He printed it out and took it back to the sofa.

After reading the document for a minute or two, he looked up at us. "Wow. This is better than I hoped. Why don't the two of you come over here and take a look at this?"

When we had settled in, one of us on either side of him, he pointed to a passage in my diary. "Read this part."

There were two figures on the porch, a man and a woman. The woman I sensed in a shadowy manner, as if she were not fully there. The man seemed mostly there, though the clearest thing about him was his strange sombras.

I had made a mistake, putting "sombras," the name of the nearby city of Las Sombras, in place of "sombrero."

"I must have been tired. Does it mean something?"

"Possibly not," Billy answered. "But you are writing about what is clear and what is not clear about your experience of these two figures, and when you get to the clearest thing of all, the sombrero, suddenly it isn't a bit clear, and something else is there, not a hat, but *sombras.* You grew up in California, right? You must know some Spanish. *Sombras* means 'shadows' or 'shades,' which is to say, *ghosts.*"

"You're making too much of it."

"This sort of thing happens all the time when paranormal investigators keep journals. Possibly significant 'mistakes' occur, as if the ghosts were slipping messages into their writing."

"But this example is a little different," Shy observed, "because Mike didn't have any idea that there were ghosts around. This might be my grandfather's way of telling him that there were."

"And there's more," Billy said. "Read on."

Though the figures were eerie, I was not afraid (afraid always now). They seemed to be inpouring me.

I had to laugh. "You guys are making a believer out of me. I meant 'imploring' of course. But I guess that fellow in the big hat was *inpouring* himself, or pouring himself into, my personal diary."

Shy spoke again, excited. "Look at the way the ghost writer seems to catch onto the word 'afraid,' which you had just typed and used properly. He then repeats the same word to launch his own message in a parenthesis, *afraid always now.*"

The elation of discovery faded as the desperation in this message from beyond seeped into her awareness. "This is clever, the ghost is clever, but this is also . . . sad. I never knew the man who is speaking through you, Mike, but I've loved him all my life. I'm not unhappy that I was sitting with my mother while you two were eyeing each other. Still, I can't help wishing that I had been looking at Old Cabin on Thursday evening."

Billy shrugged. "What difference would it have made? What could the ghost have told you that it did not tell Mike? The message was sent and the message was received. Why don't you folks go back to your couch, so I can talk to both of you at once?"

We did, but this time we sat next to each other. I reached over and clasped her hand for a few seconds.

Billy put my diary entry aside. "After what I just saw, Mike, I gotta ask. Have you ever had anything to do with ghosts?"

"Not really."

"That doesn't mean 'not at all.' Take your time."

I thought back over my life. "I remember one thing. I was a little kid and my parents gave me my first job at the inn they owned and managed. I was supposed to clip the hedges growing on one side of the hotel. The job had always been done by a Mexican gardener named Miguel who had worked for my parents for years. He had died recently. Some of the maids and other staff people had seen his ghost in the early morning or at twilight time hovering around that particular hedge. When I started doing my clipping job, they called me *poco Miguel*, little Michael, or *Miguel viva*, Michael alive. It bothered me to the point where I often sensed someone behind me. I would turn suddenly, hoping to get a clear look at my companion, and would sometimes see a form fade into the shadows and disappear."

"So you never got a full look," Billy said. "Tell me. Did you sense that the shadowy person behind you was wearing a straw hat?"

"Actually, now that you mention it. . . . Yes, I think he did." I answered calmly, but inside my blood was running cold. Billy was right. Miguel from my childhood had some-how morphed into Angel.

"Anything else?"

"My grandfather Wilbur, father's father, lived with us for years. He enjoyed me. I loved him. He went to the hospital for a time. My mother was supposed to take me to visit him, but it didn't work out. The next day he died. The day after that I was walking down a corridor of our house and passed a little room that we used as a den. The furniture was comfortable, and we kept books, magazines, and newspapers in there. My granddad loved to sit in that room. That's where he would tell me stories and talk to me about life. Anyway, I glanced in and there he was, sitting in his favorite chair, reading. He didn't look up at me. He didn't acknowledge me at all. But I was immensely comforted to find him there, and went on about my business with a deep conviction that he was all right without me and I was all right without him."

"Anything else?"

"Well, this doesn't really count as a ghostly experience, but I did write part of a horror movie."

"Really? Which one?"

"*Fog-Bound*. My ex-wife produced it, and I did a light rewrite, uncredited. Mostly I shaped the ending."

"That was a good flick, and I loved the ending. It showed the dangers of trying to empathize with ghosts. They know damn well the effects they have on the living, and they use everything at their command to trick you and bend you to their purposes. Could there be more?"

"That's all I can think of right now."

"Look, Mike. My quick assessment? I don't think you're a medium. You're not remotely a medium. But I do think you're what is sometimes called a 'sensitive.' You register ghosts. Paranormal things happen around you. I never saw the old couple in the Griswold cabin. I believed in them. I sensed they were capable of appearing. But they never appeared to me, and I spend years playing in their vicinity and was no doubt full of puppy love for their granddaughter. But those ghosts appeared to you, a stranger. They must have found you friendly and receptive."

Billy told us that once, during the early days of his ghost extermination business, he had tried working with a local medium named Judy Hayden. His main gripe with her was that she cared more about empathizing with the (in her view) emotionally damaged ghosts than ridding Ghost Killers clients of their supernatural afflictions.

"Some people are born to understand ghosts, to feel their sense of injustice, to sympathize with their sense of unfinished business. Mediums come on like priestesses of otherworldly soap opera. They generally want to appease the ghosts in some manner out of the hope that they will then abandon their vendettas and sink into non-being, or even better walk down that fabled tunnel with the bright light at the end and crowds of waiting relatives and loved ones. Not me. I was born to get rid of the things. I grant there are a rare few benign ghosts like your grandparents, Shy. But the ones you get called about in my business are overwhelmingly creatures of malice. They mean no good to the living. They thirst for vengeance, and they're jealous of the living, who eat and drink and feel warmth. Empathizing with them is dangerous—dangerous for you, dangerous for the team. I think a ghost is someone who botched death the first time around. Why? Loved life too much? In a tiny percentage of cases, yes. More likely because they didn't want to leave this life without doing damage to it. The second time around I want to make sure they get death right. I don't want to understand them any more than I need to in order to usher them out of this life.

"There are two ways to go. You either convince a ghost to leave this world completely. Sounds like paranormal suicide, but isn't, when you think about it. You want the ghost to give its full consent to the death that up to now it has resisted. Second, you kill, you terminate a recalcitrant ghost. You give it no choice. You make its half-life so miserable than it is propelled out of it into true death. Whatever that may be. I think true death is one hundred percent death. You may believe in another world beyond this one. It doesn't really matter so far as ghosts are concerned. We can agree, I hope, that they don't belong in *this* world, and are in fact its mortal enemies."

Cheyenne was a little convinced, a little amused, a little indignant. "Working with Judy Hayden was not exactly giving mediums a fair chance. She's always been impossible. I mean, other girls would dislike your clunky bracelet and tell you so, but Judy Hayden would warn you with desperate insistence that its 'negative energy' had laid you open to psychic attack from some pissed-off 'entity' in the 'paranormal realm.'"

"I see your point," Billy replied. "I was really just trying to tell Mike that I looked forward to working with a sensitive and am glad that he isn't a medium. Think about how Mike related to the ghost of your grandmother Consuela, Shy. He sensed that she was less forcefully present than Angel. Whatever Angel feared had already partially or entirely happened to Consuela. A medium would probably have gotten caught up in elaborating Consuela's suffering. Mike registers what we need to know, but doesn't take up one vortex of pain to the detriment of the overall picture. That's what Judy did."

Through most of this I was thinking over what Billy had said about understanding spirits vs. getting rid of them. The point seemed sound to me, crisp and clear. Lately there had been legions of horror movies where the haunters and lurkers were portrayed as victims, the exploited and the silenced, just waiting for a human champion of compassion to take up their cause before they could head down that scary tunnel to that happy light.

"Anyway," Billy continued, "Quicksilver Canyon is another place that I have been dying to investigate for years now. The entrance to that arroyo is closer to Old Cabin that to any other structure on the Griswold Ranch."

He turned back to Cheyenne. "Unless you've put up a new shop or something. I haven't been allowed on the ranch in over fifteen years."

"You're right," Cheyenne said. "The closest building is Old Cabin."

"Maybe your Dad will be in a mood to change his mind now. He always feared that my presence would somehow shoo his ghosts away. I would stick a Tri-Field Meter in their ectoplasmic faces, or something like that, and they would flounce off somewhere else where they would not be offended by the gadgets of the modern world. But anyway. Your mother's mental state could be related to the Old Cabin turmoil. That's one of our emergencies."

He kept speaking as he fetched a drink from the Coke machine. "Our second urgent problem is the appearance of a new serial killer." As he took his seat again, he turned to me. "I don't know how much you've been told about Dieter

Thorson, our local Black Ash Canyon Killer from the early 1990s."

I was aware of Shy looking at me as I answered. I got the unspoken message. Honest up until this moment, I was to say nothing of her tears last night, her reluctance to speak of Dieter Thorson. "Well, not much. His first victim was found at one of Ben Griswold's oil wells. That's about it."

"Found shot in the back of the head with a .22 pistol, to be exact. The corpses of his next two victims, also women, were found in Quicksilver Canyon after Dieter was shot by the police. They were killed with a knife, pretty horribly, just like the body found Friday morning at the Fountain of Sorrow. Where Dieter actually did those two final killings remains unclear. The police eventually found his car hidden in the woods of Santa Rosita State Forest. That's fifteen miles of rough terrain to the north. He had carted both the women, perhaps both of them already dead, into the back entrance of Quicksilver Canyon and was camping there, working on his notebooks."

Billy and Shy locked eyes momentarily. "Cheyenne and I were just ten-year-old kids at the time. Despite all the warnings to be careful and not to wander off from adult supervision, we tried to have fun with the Black Ash Canyon murders. We played serial killer at the Fountain of Sorrow, pretending to be stalking our next victim. I would offer Shy a candy bar to walk with me in the woods. She would sneak up behind me and put a lasso around my body."

"Is this really relevant?" Shy asked.

"It gives Mike the flavor of those days. We had always been under a strict ban concerning Quicksilver Canyon. There's a dangerous old mercury mine up there, and other hazards, and both of Shy's parents warned us repeatedly not to play there. But in a couple of weeks we got tired of the oil well and started investigating Quicksilver Canyon. The first afternoon we found some odd things. A crumpled piece of paper in particular. I opened it. In black pen was written "Why I should" and then, switching to a red pen, "change," and that word change was all doodled up so that flames shot from the letters, and the word was boxed in with a black rectangle formed of chain links. We also found some food wrappers and a lipstick tube.

"We came back the next morning. Maybe fifty yards into the side canyon we smelled a campfire. I think I was the one who stopped us in our tracks right there, and whispered that we had to go back home, quickly and silently. Is that how you remember it, Shy?"

"Yes. I was having fun. I wanted to keep on exploring."

"I called for my Daddy to come and get me, and we went into the police station in Lassiter Springs. I told my story and showed them the paper with the writing on it and the lipstick tube. Three policemen went up into Quicksilver Canyon that afternoon to investigate. Dieter resisted, fired at them. In the ensuing fight Dieter Thorson was shot in the throat and soon bled to death. The cops found the two bodies with whom he shared his camp grounds.

"Luckily, the role that Shy and I played in ending Thorson's reign of terror was kept out of the media. Police said they had acted on a tip, but never named their source. Details came out about Dieter's troubled childhood, the stories he had begun to tell his chums about how easy it was to drive around the area and pick up young women, especially college girls. All three of his victims attended colleges in this area. It began to be rumored—or so I learned, a few years later-- that Dieter had left elaborate notebooks about his crimes and their meanings. Again, Shy and I were just kids and this information touched us only vaguely. I remember some older bully at school who one day pulled out a red-covered notebook and asked me for my address so he could enter it in his 'kill list.' I would later learn that, a month after Dieter Thorson's death, three of his mysterious notebooks appeared on the internet. Could have been posted by someone in the police department or conceivably a reporter. Some of the postings, not all, were taken down by court order a month later. By then lots of people around here had downloaded them. Four years after Dieter's death, copies were loaned me by a farmer, an old family friend outside of Lassiter Springs.

"There was a Black Notebook devoted to rambling thoughts about women, murder, God and the Devil—a shapeless meditation on the cosmic vibrations of serial killing. The Blood Notebook, which had caught the interest of my confused schoolyard bully, was a shorter work about why he had switched his murder method from a gun to a knife. The entities he had contacted in the spirit world preferred the older weapon. Modern forensics made bullets easier to trace than knife wounds. More importantly, sharpness and cutting were more primal than shooting and wounding. You had to see your victim up-close. The hilt was in your hand and you handcrafted the blade's effects. Stabbing was more manly than shooting. There was a fruitcake passage about how shooting was like cumming on a woman's body from a distance, whereas stabbing was like fucking. And so on."

That rang a bell, and I broke into his narrative. "A nutcase writer named Norman Mailer said something similar after he stabbed his wife. Something like 'So long as you use a knife, there's some love left.' I remember one of my University of Virginia professors telling me about it. I think he thought it was clever."

Billy shook his head in disgust. "Sign of the times, I suppose. Dieter also left a Ghost Notebook. That was the most interesting of them to me, but also the least coherent. He didn't have a human mentor. He didn't have a spirit guide, or any contact with a medium. Everything was spun out of his own thoughts. He had long mental conversations with some spirit he called the Chain Man, or in some places The Inchworm. He thought this Chain Man ghost was teaching him true precision, some form of discipline or method that he had always lacked before. I thought of course about the word 'change' on the paper I found in Quicksilver Canyon, surrounded with a rectangle of chain links.

"In the years to come, as I learned more about ghosts and had some real experiences with them, I wondered if Dieter Thorson had been possessed. Let me just tell you a bit of what I think about ghosts."

Most paranormalists agreed, according to Billy, that ghosts can only rarely harm human beings. They can't shoot you. They can't stab you. They can't kill you. They can knock you about, maybe bruise you. They can scare the bejesus out of you. But there are very few real-life accounts of ghosts killing someone or causing serious bodily harm. They are not that powerful. Some paranormalists believe that even materializing, manifesting themselves to living beings, requires an enormous output of energy. Few ghosts can sustain a materialization for very long.

The kind of supernatural entity that actually can, in the modern paranormal literature, harm a human being is called a demon, not a ghost—the difference being that a ghost was once alive on this earth, whereas a demon never was. As a result of this distinction, all the really dangerous stuff, including the possession of a human being by an invading spirit, got categorized as religious phenomena. Faced with demonic possession, you needed a priest, not a ghost hunter.

"I believe in ghosts," Billy declared. "I've seen them, I've fought them. But I do not believe in demons. That requires an entire religious context that I find frankly incredible. But there is such a thing as possession. I've seen that too, and I've fought against that. How is possession possible if there are no demons, no scorned aspects of God, no bad deities taking revenge on the gods and their followers? Ghosts *can* violate and possess a human personality. Nothing else makes sense, not to me. Ghosts, as the paranormalists rightly say, are not that powerful. By possessing a human being, they can gain back some of the powers of the living. They can shoot. They can stab. They can take revenge. They can also enjoy again the ability to move about at will."

Ghosts, Billy maintained, are territorial. They have a haunt. They hang around the place they lived or the place they died. They draw what little power they command from this familiarity. This could explain why ghosts often frequent castles, for such buildings over long stretches of time hold onto their ancient trappings and decorations. Add everything up, and possession is a ghost's ultimate power trip. But, he added, only a very few ghosts are powerful enough to attempt it. That was the good news.

I thought I saw where Billy was going. "So we are dealing with this exceptionally powerful kind of ghost. Dieter Thorson might have been possessed by such a spirit. And this new serial killer . . . might be possessed by Dieter's ghost?"

"That's my initial suspicion, yes. Dieter began with a gun and had to change to a knife. This killer has repeated Dieter's first crime, placing the body at the same spot, but skipping the gun phase. He has the perfect weapon, the knife, from the beginning. He's not just a copycat. He's a pupil."

I nodded. "But he *could* be just a copycat. As you say, those notebooks are still on the internet and there are many copies in circulation. He might be disturbed enough to read them, admire the genius of the author, and try to better his guide."

Billy nodded in agreement. "That's exactly right. So where are we? If this new serial killer is possessed by the ghost of Dieter Thorson, he might know that you and I, Shy, were partially responsible for Dieter's death. Ghosts are vengeful, and he might want to settle that score. The first emergency doesn't bode well for the Griswolds either. Good ghosts evicted from Old Cabin. Has anything taken their place? I think that you and your family, Shy, are in real danger. The police can't help, either. They would never understand things in this fashion."

Shy looked down, and shook her head. "Will we ever be finished with our childhood games, Billy? We seem to heading for another round."

"You're right, old friend. We started in on both of these cases as children. They are so woven into our lives at this point that they seem like fate." He turned my way. "Mike, you didn't wander into this on purpose. But you're here, a part of it. You may be our ace in the hole. You strengthen us, I honestly sense that. We're all here, a part of it. Let the spooks beware. We're"—his voice was booming now, full of old-time Lassiter authority—"*the new Ghost Killers.*"

He gave us our assignments. Shy was to talk her father into letting Billy return to the Griswold Ranch to investigate Old Cabin and Quicksilver Canyon. It ought to be done ASAP. We could rest tomorrow. On Monday morning, however, Billy wanted to lead us into Quicksilver Canyon. I had a job too.

"I was interested in your visit with Solly Barlow. His dog was nervous, sensing that something unusual was happening. I think Solly sensed it too. That iron horseshoe he has mounted as a doorknocker? There's an old belief, going all the way back to the Middle Ages, that iron horseshoes protect a dwelling from being entered by the devil. Solly's afraid, all right, and he feels that the danger is supernatural. I scarcely know the man. He was around now and then in the old days when Shy and I played together, but he had no real interest in us. I want you to visit him again, and tell him what we are doing and why we are doing it. Then I want you to ask him to join our team. He's seen a lot of history at the Griswold Ranch. He has a dog that senses ghosts. He has private means and major connections to the oil industry. Who knows? Some of that may come in handy. I've got an ace in the hole. I've got a queen. I think I could use a king or a jack to go with them."

"I'll do it. One more question, though."

"Fire away."

"Where did you get that jacket you had on when you came in?"

"A Japanese website. I'll write it down for you."

He scribbled on a magazine page, tore it off, and handed it to me.

"Thanks."

"It's a small factory. They put you on a list. You may have to wait years for a Blackhawk jacket."

I suspected it wouldn't be easy. Nothing was going to be easy.

# CHAPTER SIX

On Monday at noon four Ghost Killers met on the bank of Outlaw Creek.

Solly Barlow had joined Cheyenne, Billy, and me. Hughes crouched calmly at the new member's side.

I had visited him yesterday during the morning rains. It took some cajoling, it took some seducing, but Barlow finally admitted that through the years he had sometimes seen mysterious shapes wandering the woods at night. Lately he had observed increased activity among these silent wraiths. Whereas before their appearances had been confined to the night, now he glimpsed them in the morning and evening. A month ago he had handcrafted the horseshoe door-knocker to thwart any supernatural intrusion into his home.

As for throwing in with the Ghost Killers, he was not a joiner. I argued that he would not be able to stave off these spirits on his own, that in the end he and Hughes would have to move away. This argument finally swayed him. Billy was right. Solly had been feeling lonely and vulnerable in his Creekside Chalet.

Ben Griswold's ban on Billy Steele had been lifted. I had been invited to breakfast with the Griswolds that morning, and had been present when Billy came by to pay his respects to Ben and Valentina. Valentina remained in her bedroom, sometimes with Cheyenne for company, save for one appearance. She walked into the living room soon after Billy's arrival and stared at the newcomer. "You're not alive either, Billy Steele," she finally said to him. "You should be ashamed of yourself for thinking so."

Ben, however, greeted his daughter's old playmate with a polite caution. Finally Billy broke the ice by discovering, just as I had last Thursday, the pile of *Wings* comic books on Ben's book shelves. Pretty soon the two of them were talking about how good the short stories were in the center pages of the Golden Age aviation comics, old styles in cockpit gauges, and the design flaws of the Mitsubishi fighter planes in World War II. Billy was back onboard so far as Ben Griswold was concerned.

A few trickles of water ran down the creek from Sunday's rain. I hoped we would find the symbol at the entrance to Quicksilver Canyon intact. At this point the flow was not strong enough to be doing much damage. But I suspected the waters had been higher yesterday, during and just after the rain. Another worrying factor was the tributary joining the stream at the side canyon. I tried to push the whole subject out of mind. We would know before long.

It was a chilly day. Billy Steele, wearing a green military-issue field jacket over a black turtleneck, distributed equipment to the team from a large canvas bag on the ground before him. LED lanterns came with a warning. "It is notorious among ghost hunters that anything electrical, no matter how powerful the batteries are, tends to malfunction around spirits."

"Does that hold good with wrist watches?" Solly asked.

"Oh yes," Billy assured us. "Next time we go out, if you want to guarantee yourself a working watch—which is indeed a useful thing for all of us to have—look around for an old one with a spring winding mechanism. The same is true of thermometers or compasses. Stay away from anything electric, anything digital. But as far as light is concerned, these will give us a backup."

He reached in the bag and began handing out night vision goggles.

"Just like on TV," Shy said.

"Snazzy," I chimed in. "Our ratings will go up. If they had known what they were doing in 1931, they'd have shot *Dracula* in black and green, not black and white."

"Hey," Billy said, "I'm sick of those pretentious TV ghost shows too. I don't carry thermometers. Sure, cold spots often signal the presence of ghosts, maybe because, as has been speculated, they draw on thermal energy. But I don't need some fancy device to tell me I'm shivering. I also don't need an electro-magnetic field meter to tell me that a ghost may be preparing to materialize. I'll see him if he does. I don't put any stock in those ridiculous sound recording devices that supposedly capture ghosts speaking or conversing in the static. I've listened to hours on end of that crud, and never heard anything but annoying waves of static. You hear someone being raped or murdered? That's your fantasy, bub. It seems to me a clear case of aural Rorschach. But the goggles are another matter. They're simple and non-electronic. They don't malfunction. They might save you from a world of hurt if your lantern suddenly goes out."

Cheyenne nodded and stood at attention. "Got it, Sarge."

"Now," Billy continued, "for some firepower." He handed out opaque plastic bags full of something loose and grainy. "I'm giving each of you a couple handfuls of rock salt. Don't get the wrong idea. It's been used against ghosts and supernatural creatures for centuries. But it probably won't work. I had a couple of cases where it did work, or seemed at least to slow the spirit down. What you do, then, is throw some at them . . . and hope. People believe a ghost cannot pass over a salt barrier. If you were cornered, you might do a line of the stuff and then hope with all your might."

I couldn't help myself. "So I should take this with a grain of salt?"

"Frankly," Shy said, "I'm not sure this salt is worth its salt."

Even Solly had a go at this one. "After I throw it at the ghost, do I have to throw it over my left shoulder?"

Billy was pretending to get a kick out of these wisecracks, but I sensed that he had heard them before, and was helping us get through a phase. "Think of this as weapons-grade salt. I get it from an old mining operation east of San Bernardino in the Mojave Desert. Like I say, I've seen it work a couple of times. I've seen it fail. If you know of anything better to use against ghosts, let me know."

He waited. None of us knew of anything better.

"As a matter of fact, *I* know of something." He handed us another round of opaque plastic bags. These were heavier. "This is iron. Mr. Barlow knows about this stuff. An aluminum horseshoe wouldn't have had a chance of working, would it Solly? The ancients thought of iron as the blood of the earth, and that of course is where the dead are buried. The dead don't have warm blood like the living. Death is cold. So the idea got around that cold iron, iron that had never been smelted or felt the heat of the forge, frightened or deterred or wounded the dead."

I tried again, striking a kung fu pose. "Burn with my salt! Freeze with my iron!"

"Again," Billy said immediately, not about to let the joking spread this time, "it probably *won't* work. But in my experience it has a better chance of working than salt. I get my iron ore from a deposit in Profumo Canyon outside San Luis Obispo. I cold-forge iron rods in my own shop, then break the rods down into filings. Again, just toss a handful at a materialized spirit. You've got the right stuff, honest-to-God old school cold-forged iron. It might work."

He recommended that, if we had deep side pockets in our jackets, we should open the plastic bags and pour out the contents, one per side. It might be important to remember which was where. The easiest way to remember that was to put the most powerful substance, iron, on the most powerful side. Iron on the right, if we were right-handed, and salt on the left. We all turned out to be right-handed, save for Billy. He was our only lefty.

"One more thing," Steele said, "the most important thing. I'm the leader. You can ask questions. I will often encourage group consultations. But I give the orders. For the good of the team, every one of you have to obey me,

quickly and to the letter, no matter how pointless or wrong-
headed the order may seem. Let that sink in, and we'll be on
our way."


We walked downstream two abreast, Billy and Solly in
the lead, Cheyenne and I behind them. As we approached
the quartered circle, I could see that a pool of water had
indeed formed in that section of the creek. I hoped the
skewer or spike—or whatever that iron thing in the center
was—remained in place.

We stared at the circle of rocks. The temperature went
down. Hughes began to bark. Finally I stepped into the
muddy stream bed. "Might as well see if the centerpiece is
still here." I bent down and reached into the pool. My
forefinger slipped into a metal hoop. Yes! I pulled the odd
thing up and handed it, still wet and cold and dripping, to
Billy. "What do you make of that?"

He looked it over and passed it to Solly. "I don't know,"
Billy said. "It's like you said. A long spike with a loop at one
end. I don't know what the hell it is."

Solly stepped forward, taking over. "I do."

"Tell us," Billy said.

"The design looks like a gun sight, pointed at that canyon. It's not. It's cross-hairs in a circle, but from a telescope, not a gun sight. This is a surveyor's mark. An X in a circle marks the spot on old survey maps—the boundary corners, the landmarks, the benchmarks, the places from which the surveyor's major triangulations were measured."

Solly referred to a Sarah Palin flap from 2010. On her internet site she posted a list of democrats being "targeted" by the GOP in the forthcoming elections. There was a map of America in which the states of these politicians were marked with symbols similar to the one in Outlaw Creek. The press, assuming the symbols were views from a gun sight, had another go round on their great theme of her crudity and lowness. Palin and her staff claimed that the symbols were surveyor's marks. This explanation was greeted with much derision in the press. She might well have meant the symbols to be the cross-hairs of a rifle's sight. But the defense was not laughably outrageous. Coordinates in a circle were indeed used to designate key spots on old surveyor's maps. Solly was familiar with old maps from the various oil fields where he grew up and later worked.

"This thingamajig is the clincher," he said, holding up the iron centerpiece. "It's a surveyor's arrow from the nineteenth century. When a team had stretched out their chain, they drove this spoke into the ground to mark the spot where the pole should be placed next."

"Interesting," I conceded. "But here the mark seems to be used as a kind of road sign, pointing to a route."

"And I think its purpose was immediate, not long term," Billy proposed. "A good rain might have dislodged the rocks and swept the arrow away. This sign, this indicator of a route, if that is what it is, was meant to do a job now or in the near future. Let's forge ahead."

The first thirty or forty yards were fairly steep. We were reluctant to use the rocks for leverage, since it looked as if they might easily be dislodged. Once we overcame this tiny summit, the canyon rose at a more comfortable rate. At perhaps a mile in we rounded a bend, and a vista opened up to the west along a narrow ridge. Above us, to the east, was a thick ledge. Fifty yards to the north, Quicksilver Canyon came to a dead end. Solly and Hughes walked on in that direction.

The three of us rested. Two hawks soared in the swirling winds above this maze of mountains and ravines. I wondered if the birds hunted in pairs. Could I have seen the same two hawks on the morning I first laid eyes on this arroyo?

"There's something here," Solly shouted.

We walked into the deep shadows at the close of the canyon. Solly was standing over an outcrop of fairly smooth rock, pointing at his discovery. Set into the rock face was a round brass plate six inches in diameter. The plate was engraved, and despite the effects of weathering, most of the writing could be deciphered. A date, 1915, was the most prominent bit of information. The marker had been placed by Golden State Land and Title Trust, authorized by the Surveyor General of the State of California.

"I suspect this represents a boundary corner of what is now the Griswold Ranch," Solly suggested. "From here they had good sighting to the west. They might have triangulated the western boundary of Griswold Ranch from here."

Billy nodded, looking down the western ridge. "Or, same difference, the eastern boundary of Steele Ranch."

I remembered something Ben had told me my first day in Black Ash Canyon. "Wasn't that boundary in dispute at some point?"

Billy laughed. "It sure as hell was. My father has never gotten over it. This canyon was originally part of our spread."

"Actually," Shy said, "the ranches came later, as a result of this survey or one like it. In 1915 this territory belonged to United Oil. The Southern Pacific Railroad had sold them the whole canyon a decade earlier. This marker must come from the oil company survey that defined saleable divisions in the canyon."

But Steele had lost interest in the surveyor's marker. He was craning his neck to look over the rock face behind us. "I think we could climb to the ledge from this angle. What do you think?"

I looked at the sky. There were now four hawks circling above us. We started climbing toward the ledge. It was slow going, over ground that was not only steep but loose. Pebbles and hard dirt showered down the incline as we ascended. Billy reached the ledge before the rest of us, and gave us a hand as one by one we joined him there. It was a nice wide ledge, ten feet or more in most places.

When we were all up there, I saw a group of shadows wheeling on the cliff face. I looked up, where, against a backdrop of utter silence, something incredible had been taking shape. The sky was dark with swarming hawks, uncountably many, hundreds. They floated within a single vast communal gyre, wide in the unbounded air above the mountains, then narrower and narrower inside the tapering walls of Quicksilver Canyon. Hawks spiraled slowly from the top to the bottom of this cone, then slowly back up to the top. We were all staring at it, mesmerized by a rare natural wonder. The exception was Hughes, who whimpered and barked.

I became aware that the cone of hawks was shifting our way. Its outer edge was about fifty yards from us. I heard shrill angry calls. Then forty yards. Then thirty. Hughes barked defiance. I remembered reading somewhere about hawks attacking dogs. Maybe those were smaller dogs? Hughes was a full-sized German shepherd. The wing span of the largest hawks looked to be over five feet. One broke formation and scouted the air within ten feet of my head. I saw its black and yellow eyes. I saw its legs stretched out, talons ready to clutch.

"Let's get out of here!"

We headed along the ledge. There were some places where, due apparently to erosion, the plateau shrank to three or four feet, and we had to pass in single file. The hawks were much closer now, adding immeasurably to our confusion. They knew we were big, alive, earthbound. They knew we were lumbering mammals, not at all like them, sleek and compact and wind-riding. They screeched their contemptuous hoarse rasps at us as they wheeled by. I yearned for a clump of large boulders, trees to duck behind, any respite at all from our vulnerable exposure.

We rounded a corner and spontaneously came to a halt. A choice waited twenty yards ahead, where a dark cave opened in the rock. Its mouth, though uneven, still seemed man-made, more like a square than a flowing natural shape.

"That must be the old mercury mine," Billy said.

"I'm just hoping that two of these hawks don't have a nest in there," Shy said, implying that we would take shelter in the spot. "Solly? Mike?"

"I'm game," Barlow managed, out of breath.

That left me. "What else can we do? But to tell you the truth, I don't like the look of that cave one damn bit. I don't think the hawks do either. They're giving the entrance some berth."

A few feet away from the cave mouth, all of us sensed the likely reason for its shunning by the hawk swarm. The cave stank of sulphur fumes.

"That's *foul*," Shy said, covering her mouth.

"I suppose you don't have gas masks?" I asked Billy.

"Not this trip," he replied. "Get your lights out, and in case they fail make sure you know where your night goggles are."

We entered into a surprisingly spacious antechamber. There were signs that the old mine had been inhabited in the past—a rock-lined pit with evidence of ashes and a half ring of boulders surrounding it, smooth enough for human beings to sit on in some comfort or stack their belongings on. The shaft seemed to extend inward from the left side of the chamber. I shined my light in that direction. There was rubble back there, and a low opening. I took a few steps toward the opening. The sulphur fumes were stronger. It was distinctly colder back there.

A giant rattlesnake a foot wide rose before the opening, hissing and furious, and struck at me. "Jesus!" I heard another cry as I fell back. My head fell on soft turf, but I banged my left shoulder against a rock. My lantern had gone careening into the side of the cave. It struck rock and went dark. Staring up into near darkness, I sensed another light wink off. Someone else had seen that horrible snake.

Billy was there in a flash and helped me to my feet. "Quick! Shine your light back there!" I told him, pointing to the area I had been about to explore. There was no sign of the snake. Barlow had also seen the apparition, and he too had fallen and damaged his lantern. We briefly compared notes. "I knew it wasn't real, couldn't be real, but it fright- ened me to the core," Solly said. He had scraped an elbow, but was otherwise unharmed. Billy suggested that I don my goggles, but I didn't feel able to face an unfamiliar green palette.

The Ghost Killers gathered their courage and approached the back of the cave. The opening turned out to be a hole. Fetid sulphur gases rose from it. Billy picked up a good-sized rock and pitched it through the opening. There were several long seconds of silence followed by a splash.

"I'm just guessing," Billy said, "but this looks to be a secondary tunnel, dug to see how thick the ore seam was. The main shaft was below us. We didn't see the entrance because the miners dynamited it. That was the obvious safety hazard. They left this short exploratory tunnel open. But in time the floor collapsed into the main shaft below, which had become flooded."

As he spoke with such calm rationality, I watched with mounting terror as an inky form gradually and inexorably took shape. Shy clutched my arm. I wasn't alone in my fixation. Her grip hurt my bruised shoulder, but it was no time to be fixated on my own aches and pains. A dark humanoid body took shape from the shadows cast originally by our two remaining lanterns.

Billy finally noticed it and instantly ceased explaining how the tunnel had come about. The back of the cave was now pure light and the gaping opening to the suphurous waters below an outlined blackness. The shadows seemed to have left their hollows and contributed what substance they had to the roiling man-form.

A single short word echoed in the cavern. "*Death*!"

I reached into my right-side pocket, the powerful side. This was no time to play around with a low dosage! I had lost some of the filings as a result of my fall. But I scooped up the remaining cache. Before I could toss them at this scarecrow of shadows, I saw Billy's right arm swing forward like a man throwing a horseshoe. A little cloud of rock salt sailed through the air and into Mr. Shadows. There was a brief burp, like a gas fire igniting, and the shadows shot back to their usual recesses. My hail of filings, too late, shot into the void. I didn't hear a splash. I didn't hear a thing.

When we emerged from the cave, the skies were clear, not a hawk in sight, and the winds from the canyon were indescribably sweet. We walked on a ways to distance ourselves from all traces of the mine's putrid fumes.

We neophyte Ghost Killers looked to our leader for explanations. I spoke for the three of us. "What the hell was that, Billy? Have we seen a ghost?"

"No. Not directly, at least. That was arranged by a ghost, but I think it was like a security alarm of some kind, in that it happened automatically and in his absence. When Mike and Solly started toward the back of the chamber, they tripped a switch, or the equivalent of a switch, and the snake hallucination played. That part of it seemed meant to scare away hikers or foolish children, people who had wandered unknowingly into the ghost's den. They got a damn good scare. I expect they would leave the place and never come back, and no one would believe their tale."

I knew instantly he was right.

"The second trigger, I suspect, was the stone I threw into the back cavern. That's when the shadows began to form. Is that how the rest of you experienced it?"

We all nodded. "But the security alarm analogy breaks down here, doesn't it?" I asked. "Mr. Shadows was terrifying. He frightened the crap out of me. But I think he was meant to be, in some twisted manner, *enticing*. He was showing the way."

"I agree," Billy replied. "We threw a rock, breaking the plane of the cavern's entrance. Then we were shown a black cavern mouth, surrounded by light. Mr. Shadows gave a name, death, to what lay waiting in the cavern—a grave of salty, sulphurous waters sealed in the depths of a mountain."

Understanding dawned. "That's why you threw the salt!"

"I didn't really deliberate about it. But yes, the danger being highlighted centered on salt and sulphur, and instinctively that's what I countered with. It worked too, a lot better than ever before. This clue drew me to the hypothesis of an automatic haunting-from-a-distance. If real spirits had been inside that cave, the salt would not have been so effective."

Shy was still puzzled. "You say the intended audience for the snake hallucination was hikers or kids, people that had for some random reason wandered into the mine. Who was Mr. Shadow's intended audience?"

"Your guess is as good as mine," Billy told her. His ensuing silence let all of us get to know our guesses.

My own associations were too fevered and inchoate to share with the group. I thought of the separation of dark from light in the biblical Creation. But in this version shadows had come to life. I thought of the standard picture of life's finish line, a dark tunnel with light at the end. This was a light tunnel with dark at the end, a dive platform into a pool of stinking inescapable nothingness.

Billy, still revving with purpose, looked us over. "What do you say, folks? Are you still up for a visit to Old Cabin?"

Three heads nodded. I think all of us realized that Mr. Shadows was probably living there.

# CHAPTER SEVEN

When we got back to the Griswold compound, Billy suggested we break for lunch before investigating Old Cabin. He had brought along a cooler of freshly made turkey sandwiches. I offered my cabin and front porch as a picnic area. As I fetched beers and soft drinks, Cheyenne walked over to the ranch house. Just as we were unwrapping our sandwiches, she reappeared with paper plates and a bowl of macaroni salad. Over the meal we discussed the morning's events.

"What was that hawk swarm about?" I began. "Do you see that often around here?"

"Not often," Billy replied. "But it does happen in the California fall when the birds migrate south. That was a very large swarm, however, and an amazing display of group-formation aviation."

"Is there one of those fancy words for a flock of hawks?" Cheyenne wanted to know.

"A *kettle*," Solly said. "A kettle of hawks."

I spoke again, returning to the issue that had been bothering me in the first place. "I was wondering whether there could be any connection between ghosts, or ghost security alarms, and those hawks."

"The main effect of the birds," Solly remarked, "was to drive us into the mine shaft."

"Apparently," Billy nodded. "But the giant snake hallucination was meant to drive us away. I'm not sure what the intent of the Mr. Shadows vision was. But I'm baffled as to why a ghost would induce a kettle of hawks to herd us into the tunnel, then set up a snake apparition to scare us out."

I thought I had the answer. "The hawks drove us into the mine because we were already on the ledge. They began to swarm as we were concentrating on the climb. If we had been on the canyon floor, the effect would have been different, wouldn't it? We would have left the canyon and gone back across Outlaw Creek."

"Good point," Billy replied. "There are lots of reports in the paranormal literature about ghosts possessing or influencing dogs, cats, horses, and parakeets—any animals that serve as human pets. I suppose that a particularly powerful ghost might be able to implant a wild alpha hawk with the idea that visitors to Quicksilver Canyon ought to be chased away by a big display of hawk power."

"You've mentioned several times the power of this ghost. Is that another way of saying that you have never encountered a spirit with such resources?"

"That's right, Mike. I never *have* run into anything like this. The paranormalists distinguish between a 'residual haunting' and an 'intelligential haunting.' In the first a ghost stages some traumatic event over and over. The living are made to see a betrayal or an act of violence. Presumably the ghost wants things made right, wants something done to compensate it for an old wrong. There's no fixed script in an intelligential haunting. The ghost may be friendly and imploring at times, angry and terrifying at times. But usually there turns out to be some underlying disquiet. Just as in a residual haunting, the ghost wants something heretofore covered to be uncovered. Something needs to be settled or put right. But these ghosts? What they want from the living, if they want anything, is not yet clear to me. Their power is undeniable. If my 'security alarm' analogy is correct, they can make apparitions that act in their absence. I'm guessing that Mike is right, and they can fill a canyon with hawks too."

I was finished with my sandwich. I looked around at the Ghost Killers. Then I did what I had been avoiding, and turned my gaze to Old Cabin. It stood there under the trees, its boards darker than ever. Before there had been a gloom at the edges and corners of its weather-beaten walls and roof. Now, post-fire, the gloom seemed to reside in the structure itself.

Billy took Cheyenne's hand. "I want you to sit this one out, Shy."

"Stay here? While the rest of you enter that cabin? I won't do it."

"But you must," Billy persisted, "for your own sake. The ghosts of two of your relatives have been driven from that cabin. What their fate has been, we have no idea. I can't let you risk your life on a fact-finding mission. We're not prepared to assault these ghosts. We have no strategy, no idea of *how* to assault them. If they were to harm you, or worse still possess you, I would never forgive myself. Your father would never forgive me. No, I think you better stay away from Old Cabin for now."

Solly and I indicated our agreement with this reasoning. Reluctantly, Shy agreed to wait for us at the ranch house. We walked as a group toward Old Cabin. When we came level to the ranch house, Cheyenne split off with a hug for each of us. She kissed my cheek, whispering "Take care, Mike." I wanted to kiss her back, but kept my focus on the task ahead.

I was carrying the lantern she had used in the mine. Billy had found a new one for Solly in the back of his Jeep Cherokee. He had also replenished our supply of rock salt and iron filings. The night googles were in our pockets, but we had decided that the lanterns would provide sufficient visibility.

Ben had not gone inside the cabin after the fire, but from the outside had boarded up the broken windows. He had also cleared away the fallen roof of the porch. One should have felt sorry for the old structure, having survived so many decades of wind, rain, lightning, and fire, only to be badly scorched on a misty fall morning. Maybe it was the absence of shadows from the missing porch roof or the new planks covering the windows, but now Old Cabin seemed harder and meaner, a less winning candidate for the pity and pathos due to age.

Ben, who was the last living being actually to have entered Old Cabin, remembered that the cooking and sitting had been done in a front room. There were two rooms behind that for sleeping.

We clattered onto the porch floor. There was no knob on the door. Billy pushed it. The door did not move. He put his shoulder to it, and pushed again. With a pop the door gave, and opened to the creaking of long-ignored hinges. Solly and I flipped on our lanterns and followed Billy inside. "Leave it open," Billy said. The cabin reeked of smoke and wet old wood.

Hughes began to growl, showing his teeth. Solly knelt beside the wary dog and spoke softly to him. Billy and I waved our lanterns over the front room. Everything was covered with dust and spider webs. The floor was foul with rodent droppings. At one end was an old pot-bellied stove that had once been vented in the wall. The venting had fallen over. A circular shaft of light entered the room from a hole that still held a section of venting pipe. There was a table with a few random pieces of dust-coated crockery.

"We have come to see you," Billy said in an even voice. "Can you show yourselves?"

We waited for an answer. Nothing happened.

Two doors stood in the back wall. The top hinge of the one on the right had fallen off, and the door swung out at a crooked angle. Billy pried it open. Our lanterns revealed a small bedroom with a tiny cot, at this point nothing but dusty slats. On the floor were some old books and what appeared to be a doll, now buried in dust. It had been a child's room.

"Shy's mother was raised here," Billy said, then repeated his greeting to the spirits. "We have come here to see you. Will you make yourselves visible to us?"

Seconds passed. Nothing happened.

"One room left," Billy said.

The second door opened normally and soundlessly. I wondered why the hinges didn't whine. The bed was large enough for two adults. The legs on one side had buckled, tilting the entire piece. There were two dusty spindle chairs and a large wardrobe. This, clearly, was the main bedroom. In the old days it would have absorbed a comforting heat, welcome in the brisk California nights, from the stove in the front parlour. Today it was cold.

Billy began again. "We have come to see you."

Before he got to the question about whether the ghosts could make themselves visible, a loud whisper came from the back corner of the room, near the bed. "*You have come to see us.*"

"Yes we have. You have been causing trouble."

"*You have come to see us. I am very old.*"

I thought that was it. What would Billy say now? But in seconds the ghost whisper continued, but at a higher volume that scratched my eardrums. "*I would like to see you!*"

Two shapes shot toward us from the corner. One was near me in a flash, and I knew its rage at once. A hard blow seemed to burst my bruised shoulder. I heard grunts and cries from Billy and Solly. Hughes emitted a strong string of barks, then began to whimper. I took another hit on the back of my neck, and then another on my chest, then another behind my knee, then another, then another. I went down prone on the dirty floor, groaning.

My mind was entered.

I had always imagined that I would register a presence in my mind as another and alien consciousness. I would go on with my mental business, but would feel a rustling or a tingling as the alien mind searched my scattered thoughts or memories. This was different. It was as if there were one and only one center of perception from which a mind could be experienced. The invader seized *my* perceiving center. What I thought, he learned. What I remembered, he learned. He could also call up whatever he wanted to know. The invader had wedged himself onto the mobile throne of my self-consciousness. I had to go along for the ride.

He took the measure of my private kingdom, observing its boundaries, marking its parts. The thoroughness of it was harrowing, the equivalent of a mental chill. We checked my sins and guilts along neighboring sectors of my memory. Pride. Envy. Greed. Sloth. Gluttony. Anger. Lust. I would suddenly be thinking, with him beside me, of the most appalling greedy things I had done in childhood, youth, maturity. Then we would suddenly switch to wrath, and flip through a similar inventory of embarrassing moments arranged chronologically. We viewed my adult guilts from the viewpoint of my childhood shames, then looked the other way, seeing my childhood shames from the viewpoint of adult guilts. The invader was painstaking, exacting, meticulous. Without response of all kind, he tallied my secrets and evasions—what I wished I were, what I pretended to be, what I had to admit I was. The invader took one last encompassing survey of everything, then left me.

Alone again on my violated throne of perception, I felt the weight of the invader's tracks on my mind. I felt the iron arrows he seemed to have driven into his major vantage points. I saw the ruins of my once beautiful and private mind. The sonofabitch had seen me all right, *completely*.

I cried for the little I was and for all the illusions I had lost.

I was walking. Arms were supporting me. My shoulder raged with pain. I glanced at Solly, then at Billy. "Let me rest." They stopped, allowing me to slip to my knees. Hughes scooted around in front of me and licked my face.

Soon I rose and the three of us walked on to my cabin. I sat on a porch chair. Billy brought me a glass of scotch. I thanked him, took a swig.

I gathered that Billy and Solly had been knocked around, but neither had undergone a mental invasion. I told them about it as best I could. Shy appeared, becoming upset when she saw the state I was in. Billy took her aside, obviously informing her of my ordeal.

"They say sage smoke helps," Billy said, "but as always with the recommendations of paranormalists, I make no promises." He took a small leafy stem from his jacket pocket, lit it on fire with a Zippo, and waved it around the porch. "I'll do this inside too," he said, then disappeared into Shady Grove Cabin. The sage did seem to be reviving. My mental oppression lifted slightly.

When he returned to the porch, Billy prepared to leave, stuffing lanterns and goggles into his canvas bag. Then he addressed us. "It's been quite a day. We've all got plenty to digest. I have some ideas about what we are facing here, and how we can proceed, but I need to put my thoughts in order. Would it be too soon to meet for breakfast tomorrow at the clubhouse? At nine? I'll handle the food."

We indicated our consent. He turned to me. "Mike, you're excused. My mind has never been violated and explored by a ghost, but I don't think you'll be feeling entirely yourself for a while." Entirely myself? I would never feel that again, *ever.* The invader had taken myself away from myself. "If you start feeling severely depressed, call me right away." I felt severely depressed, and I didn't feel like calling Billy. "It will get better. Time heals." How the hell could Billy Steele know if this was going to get better? Does time heal? Now and then, but mostly it corrupts and degrades. "You do have some unusual attunement to ghosts. I called you a 'sensitive.' I'm not altogether sure what that means. But that spirit could not enter my mind or Solly's mind. He saw a kind of natural openness in you, and seized on it." It had sounded rather nice, being a sensitive. With an ounce of prudence, I could have seen it for the curse it had turned out to be. "For tonight, I'll leave you in the capable hands of Cheyenne. Again, if you're not up to a breakfast meeting tomorrow, stay home and feel no guilt about it." The invader knew *exactly* what was in my mind. The effect? A staggering amplification of guilt. I wished so very much I could *feel no guilt.*

Billy headed for his Cherokee, which was parked in front of the ranch house. Solly said his goodbyes, and headed in the direction of Creekside Chalet.

Cheyenne sat down next to me.

"It was awful, wasn't it?"

"Very awful. I think I feel the way a woman is said to feel after being raped. Shamed, indescribably filthy."

"I feel bad that you got into this to help me. Then I stayed out of Old Cabin, and you went in—and look what happened to you!"

I sipped my whisky. "In the beginning, maybe I was helping you. But not any more." I gazed across the dappled shadows at Old Cabin. There must have been at least fifteen crows preening on its roof. "I gather that ghosts are specialists in revenge. Well, I know one ghost who's going to find out that the living are pretty good at revenge too."

"Could I cook you dinner?"

I took another sip. "I'd like that."

"What do you feel like?"

"Comfort food, and not much of it."

"I'll find something in our kitchen and be back within an hour."

When she left I headed for the shower. Hot, cold, very hot, cold, very very hot. I put on my most comfortable jeans and a loose flannel shirt.

Shy reappeared with a bag of ingredients. Blessedly, she also brought back a bottle of Percodan. I washed a couple down with some more scotch, and did a poor job of keeping her company while she whipped up plates of spaghetti carbonara. My shoulder felt better. I ate more than I had anticipated.

"Tell me about it," she said after dinner.

I did. By the end I was again in tears. When I had put myself back together again, we talked over the invasion.

"So this ghost called up your most regretted memories in categories? And the categories were the seven deadly sins?"

"Yes."

"And you weren't raised Catholic?"

"No."

"But Christian?"

"I suppose my family's moral assumptions must have been informed by Christian thought. But there wasn't much in the way of actual church-going. My mother tried to interest me in the local Presbyterian congregation, but gave it up after a couple of years. Sometimes friends would invite me to attend their churches."

"OK. Did the seven sins feel like an imposition?"

"Actually, my memories responded to those old sins as if they were somehow . . . built in."

"And the memories were very specific?"

"All memories are. Yeah, they were specific and even cross-referenced. When the spirit called up wrath memories, I looked at temper tantrums, at a girl I cruelly ridiculed in the schoolyard, at a little boy I bullied. Then the same schoolyard memories came up for pride, and the temper tantrums came up for envy."

"It does sound as if your conscience had already organized things in that fashion. What came up for gluttony? That's probably the most old-fashioned one, the sin least discussed these days."

"It may be little discussed as a sin, but think about all those government warnings about obesity, and the multitude of eating cults urging you to avoid this and only eat that. But what came up in my mind? Everything from gorging myself on Halloween candy to spells of drinking too much and two years in college when I screwed around with drugs."

"But the striking thing is that you had already, it would seem, connected gluttony with drug taking."

"I did. As some sort of failure to control my appetite."

"I'm beginning to think these seven old sins are profounder than people realize."

I paused for a moment. "I am too. I mean, obviously they are just an old list. You could imagine an expanded one or maybe an altogether different one. Where's hypocrisy, for example? That's a pretty prevalent fault. But the seven deadly have traction."

"And I must say, Mike, it doesn't sound as if your sins are that deadly."

This also gave me pause. And she was right. Looked at through the prism of the old Deadly Seven, I wasn't such a hard case. The various French, Italian, and Mexican chefs my parents employed at the Hidden Valley Inn gave me a good start on gluttony, though I had not scaled new heights in Los Angeles, where most of the people I knew, good modern relativists and tolerant of many diverse sins, were exquisitely weight-conscious and catty as all hell about the pudginess of others, to the point where a serious moralist might wonder if skinny chic were not itself a popular modern variety of gluttony. I recognized in myself a true God-given talent for lust, but with worthy partners and relationships of some duration, not in the way of wanton promiscuity. On the other hand, I was no more than average in greed. Sloth was not my problem, nor was envy. The invader hadn't gotten much from me in those categories.

If I had a special vulnerability in this whole area, wrath was no doubt my bête noir. I was really quite good at wrath. I liked the idea that it was dangerous when allowed to fester within, because that was such a subtle justification for letting the beast out. Few moments in emotional life could touch the thrill of a righteous indignation given full rein. That was, of course, my main strategy for overcoming the afternoon's humiliation. I would make the invader pay dearly for my defilement. And I would.

"This has been helpful, Shy. I'm beginning to draw strength from the same sin grid the invader used to humiliate me. I can make those seven no-nos work *for* me. Maybe I'm so upset because the invasion hurt my pride. When my mind was just for me and no one else could peek in, I could pretend it was sweeter and more precious than it was. It's comforting to see the invasion as a case of wounded pride. I'll get past this. My mind's still sweet and precious, just not so sweet and precious as I used to think."

"Your mind isn't just memories. You can also analyze. I bet the invader didn't touch *that*." She let the remark sink in. "I was wondering if we could use the seven deadly sins to learn about our enemy. Billy said that the dead were jealous of the living."

"Yes!" I pounded the table. "The invader is a jealous bastard. Envious, envious of us. Possession! What he did to me must be a prelude to entering me for good, possessing me. That would be the ultimate in humiliating someone's pride—to turn them into a slave! Greed, too. Ghosts must be greedy. They wouldn't make do with a natural life span. They had to have *more*."

"And wrathful too. As you said before, specialists in revenge."

"He knew what to look for in me because he knew himself."

She smiled. "Beware of that pride of yours. The ghost has known some other sinners too. You had the traditional sin grid in you half-consciously. I think it was a guiding principle in your invader. It's a medieval scheme, isn't it?"

"I think so."

"And the religion of the Middle Ages, in the West at least, was Catholic. Ergo, we know something about our ghost. At some point, when he was alive, he imbibed Catholic doctrine. I bet it was in his childhood. Sin makes a big impression on children."

"You're a fine intellectual companion, Shy, as well as a good motherer." Her smile glowed. I looked around the cabin at the darkness framed in my windows. "Will you sleep with me?" Her eyes widened. "I'm talking about real sleep. I do feel better, but God, what a day! My shoulder is still killing me. On top of all that, I have to admit I'm afraid to sleep alone in this cabin. Will you sleep alongside me?"

She laughed. "A most honorable proposal! I suppose that ghost didn't look for virtues? He might have found a few shreds of those."

I was serious. I waited.

"Well sure, you big lug. Can I borrow a T shirt?"

I awoke to the smell of smoke. I thought I was back in the darkness of Old Cabin, prone on the floor. I thought the invader was inside me again. Then I fought through all of that, slowly realizing that I was in bed beside a sleeping Cheyenne as dawn was just beginning to lighten my curtains. But the smoke was real.

It was curling in through my front doorjamb. I hurried into my shoes and forced the door open. Someone had braced the door with an old rusty plough that had decorated my front porch. The door opened outward. I was able with a few vigorous swings, hurting the hell out of my shoulder, to knock the plough over. Someone had poured my tin of charcoal lighting fluid over the front wall of the house and set it ablaze. I went back to the bedroom, got the spare blanket, and woke up Shy. Then I returned to the porch and smothered the fire.

"Another fire!" Shy said. "Can ghosts start fires?"

"It wasn't a ghost."

"Did you see the person?"

"Yes. Walking away from the cabin, but unmistakable."

"Well? Who was it?"

"Your mother."

# CHAPTER EIGHT

When Cheyenne and I arrived at the clubhouse for our working breakfast, Billy and Solly were conversing over waffles and bacon. We took seats at the picnic table while Billy poured batter onto his electric griddle.

"How are you feeling, Mike? You look better."

"I think I am. Having my mind explored was terrifying, but also cleansing. My pride took a tumble." I poured milk into my coffee. "We've had an interesting morning."

On the way over, we had considered whether to be perfectly honest with our fellow Ghost Killers about this morning's events. I could leave out Shy's presence in my bed, but the story of Valentina's fire would lose much of its force if they did not know that both of us were at risk. In the end we decided to render an honest account, and to say nothing about sleeping together unless asked. We figured that, if we insisted right away on the truth, that Shy had just been calming a frightened friend, no one would believe us.

"It isn't altogether certain," I ended, "that Valentina knew Shy was keeping me company." I said this, not because I believed it, but to delay the realization waiting just around the corner for Shy. She had a tough pill to swallow.

Billy saw through my wishful thinking. "Of course she did. These days Shy has been spending more time with Valentina than anyone else, including Ben." He turned to Shy. "You can't really believe that your mother didn't notice your absence. Surely you called home? And told your father where you were?"

Cheyenne nodded.

"She knew," Billy continued, hammering the point home. "The ghost occupying her mind knew. The same ghost, I would think, that occupied Mike's mind yesterday afternoon. We can't afford to soft-pedal this situation. It must be obvious to both of you that Valentina also set Old Cabin on fire."

Shy answered coldly. "You're saying that my mother tried to kill me, after burning out the ghosts of her mother and father?"

"That's precisely what I'm saying. What would make your mother torch Old Cabin? The ghosts of her parents had been living happily there for decades. No one had ever disturbed their dwelling. What would make her burn a cabin in which you were sleeping? Shy, your mother *isn't herself.* She yammers away about how all of us are dead, or ought to be dead, or should be ashamed to be alive. The woman has been communing with a ghost. She sees the world of the living under the shadow of death. Instead of envying the living, she talks as if she envies the dead. I told you that ghosts always are jealous of the dead. What do you suppose is the number one mental pathology among ghosts? I've seen it before. I see it here. It's for ghosts to pretend *the living envy them.* Ideas of that sort have been planted in your mother's mind."

I watched the pill go down in an expression of fear and disgust. Then she softened. The best thing to do was to hear the wisdom of the group. "What should we do? Take her some place far away from here?"

Billy rose, removed the waffle, plated it, and put it before Cheyenne. Then he poured another load of batter on the griddle.

"I thought about that, Shy. But what if the ghost goes with her? That's one of the advantages of possession. It allows a ghost to detach itself from familiar haunts. I believe that we have to do our best to figure out what is happening here in the canyon, and then bring it to an end. Moving Valentina to another place, no matter how far away, might not help her, and might make it impossible for us to solve the current crisis."

Billy opened the griddle and peeked at the next waffle. "Again, you have to be struck by the power of this spirit. When he greeted us in Old Cabin with that whisper-voice, he said that he was 'old.' Sometimes old ghosts become feeble, just like old people, and can barely materialize. But this one seems to have gotten stronger and more ambitious. The very fact that your mother, under his guidance, would act against her relatives with such a blasé obedience suggests the power involved. You would think there would be signs of resistance, regret, ambivalence. But no, not apparently. Have you observed anything along those lines, Shy?"

She shook her head. "Nothing like that. She likes to look at maps, but doesn't talk about them. She's preoccupied with old children's games. Yesterday morning, while you and Dad were talking, she wanted to play Ghost in the Cellar with me. We used to do that when I was a child. There was never a cellar in our house, so we used the barn. It was a simple game. Someone got to be the ghost, and hid in the barn. The other person would hunt for her, and the ghost would give her a big scare, or a pretended scare, since it was all in fun."

Billy put a hot waffle before me, and I reached for the maple syrup. "You and I played that sometimes," he said. "I gave you a few good scares. Remember that time I was hiding in the hayloft? I never saw anyone get down a ladder that fast."

That earned a brief smile. But Shy got right back to her story. "Anyway, when the game came up yesterday, I was struck with the fact that she wanted to be the ghost. When mother and I played Ghost in the Cellar in my childhood, I was *always* the ghost."

Billy topped off his coffee cup, and sat down. "I can't help but wonder if there isn't some other reason, besides the strength of the ghost, for her compliance. Angel and Consuela, her mother and father, died in a fire. Isn't that right?"

"Yes. In 1960, five years before my uncle Lars Griswold died and my father inherited the ranch. My parents didn't marry until 1965, though they had been in love for years before. I didn't come along until 1982. Late babies run in the family. Consuela didn't have mother until she was in her forties. In any case, that fire back in 1960 was ancient history to me."

"Tell us what you know about it," Billy coaxed.

"It was in the fall, not the summer, so my father wasn't living at the ranch. Lars was in town getting supplies on that day. Mother never talked about it. As best I know, there was a brush pile against one side of the barn. Lars had been meaning to clear it away. Maybe lightning struck it. Who knows? It was my grandmother's habit to bring Angel his lunch in the saddlery shop, which was in the barn, and eat there with him. There were a couple of cots in the workshop, and after lunch they would lay down together and have a brief siesta. A fire swept through the barn, killing my grandparents. Their burned bodies were found on the ashes of their cots. A surrounding stand of trees caught fire, and the blaze moved on to the ranch house. When Lars got back from town, the fires were still burning. He found my mother in tears, carrying buckets of water from the pump and throwing them at the flaming house."

Billy spoke in a quiet voice. "Where was your mother when the fire started?"

"Playing, I believe."

"Shy. She has started two fires. The ghost fiddling with her mind is no doubt a real bad ass. But I have to wonder if there is not a certain . . . predisposition in her. Is there any possibility that Valentina had something to do with the *first* fire that killed her parents? How old was she?"

"Let's see. She was born in 1943, and must have been sixteen or seventeen."

"Playing. . . . Look, Shy, I don't know what happened in 1960. Do any of us? Only your mother would *know*. But if she had started that fire, perhaps inadvertently, it would explain a lot. There has always been a debate over whether a hypnotist, even when using powerful drugs, can make a subject commit an act totally contrary to their habits and inclinations. Some say yes, a good brain-washer can make an adjusted, life-affirming person commit suicide. Others ridicule that idea as, at best, a useful rumor. There are many people who like to appear more powerful than they are, and there are many people with motives for making us think others are more powerful than they are. I've always sided with the nay-sayers. It would make more sense to me that your mother has some weakness, some gnawing guilt or denial, that made her vulnerable to a command to set these recent fires."

I was thinking, with relief, that this brainwashing ghost hadn't found anything like that in my mind.

Shy nodded in resignation. "I see your point, Billy. But if it is true, the poor woman! To live so long with the burden of having been responsible for your parents' death!"

That would be a truly heavy burden, I reflected. Taking the lives of your parents, a complete reversal of them having given you yours.

At this point Solomon Barlow, the most taciturn of the Ghost Killers, took the floor. "The ghost must have convinced her that the first fire, the one that burned her parents, was a good deed. It made dead people, which seems to be a fine thing to her current way of thinking. That's what's really frightening."

We stopped talking, and let it all sink in. Our ghost had an evil frame of mind. Pure evil.

Billy topped off his coffee cup again, took a deep breath. Then he started in on The Big Picture.

We had encountered two new ghosts in Old Cabin. Their former lair must have been Quicksilver Canyon, presumably in the abandoned mercury mine. They had clearly pressured Angel and Consuela to complete their imperfect deaths. A kind of road marker, a surveyor's iron arrow at its center, had led the couple back into Quicksilver Canyon. The marker had again been the work of Valentina, who had probably finished building the symbol just before I passed her that Thursday morning on the bank of Outlaw Creek. Once the ghost couple had entered the abandoned mine, the vision we had seen, with Mr. Shadows presiding, showed them the way to oblivion through a dark opening surrounded by shadowless walls.

There are good places to live on this earth, places where the breezes refresh, the water tastes sweet, the views thrill, the different virtues of sun and shadow are pleasantly blended. There are also good places to die, places where death will be absolute, where ghosts won't be walking away from their corpses and even spirits can call it quits. That underground sulphur lake in Quicksilver Canyon was one of the good dying spots—a sure transit to death's finality. Billy implied that we had all sensed this fact. And we had. The back of that tunnel opened on absolute death. Consuela might have left before Angel. But the fire drove both of them to a chamber of annihilation.

The two new ghosts wanted to haunt the main compound, closer to the life of the Griswold Ranch and free from proximity to the mine's terrifying back exit. The master ghost, who boasted of his age, must also want to be nearer to Valentina, already in his thrall.

The first of the apparitions I had experienced in the mine, the giant snake, had been left to scare off anyone living who had wandered into the cave. The second, the man of shadows showing the way to death, had been set for Angel and Consuela. The Ghost Killers would not have seen that vision, Billy speculated, but for me. I had been in contact with Angel the evening before the fire, and the trace of his spirit in my mind may have tripped the second vision's start switch.

What had been the names of these ghosts? The weaker one, though still a formidable spirit, was almost certainly Dieter Thorson. After murdering one girl with a gun, Dieter had begun camping in Quicksilver Canyon and writing his three notebooks. It seemed unlikely that he had brought his camping gear to the little canyon because he found its atmosphere congenial to prose composition. He had gone to the side canyon because there his spirit guide could enter him most fully and easily. The entity Thorson called "The Chain Man" or "The Inchworm" in his *Ghost Notebook* had already been residing in Quicksilver Canyon. After the police shot Thorson, his spirit joined forces with the master spirit who had possessed him when alive.

Solly was curious about their post-life partnership. "This old or 'master' spirit possessed Dieter when he was alive and figuring out what kind of serial killer he wanted to be. Does the senior spirit still possess him now that both of them are ghosts?"

"Could be," Billy said. "But maybe he doesn't need to. He has, after all, already molded Thorson's mind. It would certainly be a drain on his powers to have to occupy both Thorson's ghost and Valentina Griswold. Nowadays, perhaps, Thorson is simply obedient to his will. He doesn't have to operate him like a puppet. He can deploy him as a falconer does the falcon. Remove his hood, shake his fist, and off Dieter Thorson goes to find a new serial killer. He may be training Thorson to possess and direct human beings. Both of them seem to share an appetite for murder."

Yes, I thought to myself, an appetite for murder, whether of innocent women or benign ghosts.

We didn't yet know the identity of the older ghost, but there were solid clues. Surveying, for example. The iron arrow. Before Shy and I arrived this morning, Billy had queried Solly about "The Chain Man," the name Dieter had given his ghostly mentor. It was an old term for one of the workers in a surveying team. While the head surveyor took his sightings from a particular position, the chainman—an unskilled job, often filled by a know-nothing boy or an apprentice—moved the chain forward to the next location, marking the spot by driving an arrow into the ground. I had stressed the impersonal thoroughness of the visitor. My mind was like a piece of topography to be mathematically modeled—the boundaries observed, the access routes noted, the sins located and measured. In a harrowing literal way, I had been mapped.

The possibility that our master ghost had been a surveyor fit with Valentina's new interest in old maps. I recalled the chain I had heard clinking inside Old Cabin when I knocked on its door Thursday morning. Billy remembered the piece of Thorson's doodling he had found as a child in Quicksilver

Canyon, where the word "change" was enclosed in a rectangle of chain links.

Shy added to this sketchy portrait of our antagonist the point we had discussed last night. Given the invader's interest in the seven deadly sins, it seemed reasonable to assume that he had learned about morality from trained Catholic priests and first explored his own moral character in a confessional.

"Convincing," Billy agreed. "So what do we do now? With regard to the new serial killer, we don't have an advantage over the police, save in one particular. We know, as they do not, that any future victims are almost certainly going to be killed in Black Ash Canyon."

Solly nodded. "Maybe we could set up a couple of surveillance cameras and monitor traffic entering from either end of Black Ash Canyon Way?"

"That won't prevent a second killing," Billy said, "but it might prevent a third one. That's what the police would do if they respected our conclusions. We'll get right on it."

I nominated myself to track down information about our master ghost. "I'm a good researcher, Billy. I know what I'm looking for—a criminally-minded surveyor with a Catholic education and some connection to Black Ash Canyon.

Using the local libraries and old newspapers, I'm confident I can learn the identity of our Mr. Shadows."

"You're the designated researcher, then," Billy said. "But we may be able to gather some more details about the master ghost if we learned how to talk to Valentina." He look toward Cheyenne Griswold. "You've been at her side in recent months as often as anyone else, Shy. I don't believe that the ghost is inside her at all times. I'm guessing she sleeps alone?"

"Correct," Shy replied. "Several years ago she asked my father to move into the guest room. She goes to bed late, usually around two o'clock, and locks the door. I've heard her walking around the room at all hours."

"That must be when the ghost comes to her, enters her mind, and releases his poisons. I have the feeling that when she says those strange and eerie things, your tendency is to change the subject to something normal, to encourage her to snap out of her death trip with soothing thoughts. And who could blame you? But it might be best for her, and certainly for our investigation, to try to engage her bizarre thoughts, to ask her *more* about them rather than replace them with normal healthy thoughts. You might even ask her directly about the fires, or where she acquired the surveyor's arrow for the Outlaw Creek marker. Thorson, of course, was possessed by the same spirit, and he was certainly not reticent about writing down his new ideas and experiences in note-books. Maybe Valentina is also eager to talk about her transformation, and is just waiting for us to learn how to turn on the spigot. Anyway, I encourage you to try to devise new ways of communicating with her. Does she have any idea what the ghost's plans are? He may not have revealed his intentions to her. Or he may have exacted vows of secrecy. But she still might tell us something useful."

Cheyenne and I had our marching orders. There was no escape for Shy. She was stuck with mothering her mother, and I liked the deft way that Billy had made that chore appear central to the investigation.

Our leader was wrapping up the meeting. "That leaves you and me, Solly. Perhaps, after we rig those cameras, you and I could work on weaponry? I have some ideas along those lines. With your background in engineering, you'd be a big help."

Solly got to his feet. "Are you talking about firearms? I've lived in Alaska and the Middle East. I know my way around guns."

"That's *one* of my ideas," Billy said. "I have others too. I'll be in touch. First of all, there's a little company in Lassiter Springs that did the security for my Ghost Killers office in

Las Sombras. I'm sure they'll have some suggestions about traffic screening."

"I have a question about weapons," Shy intervened. "I know you don't think much of Holy Water and crosses, Billy. I'm not sure I do either. But remember Pascal's wager? If there is any chance those Christian objects might work on these ghosts, why not employ them? What have we got to lose?"

Billy shrugged. "If you want to arm yourself with silver crosses and vials of Holy Water, go right ahead. Personally, I've seen them tried, but I've never seen them work. I'm going to turn out something that *does* work, at least a little bit."

Shy persisted. "But one of these ghosts might be so old that *he* believes the old religious weapons will work. Haven't doctors established the existence of a 'placebo effect'?"

"I don't think these ghosts are going to succumb to any placebo effects. But I'm not prescriptive, Sly. Like I say, arm yourself as you see fit."

Outside, I fired up my truck and started driving back to the Griswold Ranch with Shy at my side. We were about halfway there when we came upon a smooth lip of hard ground jutting out from a bend in the road. It was a spot where the few voyagers through this odd canyon could treat themselves to a sense of the whole, observing the broadening farmland to the west and the narrowing cliff faces to the east.

"Pull over," she told me.

We got out of the truck. Solly drove by, giving us a wave and honk of his horn.

When he was out of sight, Shy turned into my arms and we kissed. As the woman said, once is not enough.

"What do you say, Mike? Shall I spend tonight with you in the proper way?"

"No T-shirt?"

"No T-shirt."

"No contrary thoughts?"

"Heck no. I've been head over heels in love with you ever since you told me it was OK to be embarrassing around you."

I didn't know what to say, there was so much to say. I reverted to the practical. "I don't have anything for dinner. Shall we go out?"

"You're on. Which do you prefer, by the way? Head or heels? Or do you prefer boots?"

Since embarrassment was off the table, I did my best to answer.

We lay beside each other, all passion spent, talking quietly as our sleepiness matured.

"One thing really bothered me about Billy's analysis," Shy was saying. "A teacher of mine used to call it an *infinite regress*. We have a serial killer possessed by the ghost Dieter Thorson, who was possessed by the ghost of another vicious man. What if our master ghost had been possessed by another killer-ghost? What if *his* ghost had been possessed? What if this keeps going on in both directions, all the way ahead to Doomsday and all the way back to the beginning?"

"What a thought! I suppose it could go all the way back to Cain. He would be the first possible murderer-ghost, at least in terms of the Bible."

"Yes, the mark of Cain. It's like child abuse."

"Come again?"

"It only has to happen once, then it keeps happening. The abused child grows up and wants to abuse a child. That child grows up and. . . . We're off to the races. On and on it goes. One evil deed isn't just one evil deed. It belongs to a perpetuating chain of evil deeds."

I glanced at Shy as she lay beside me, staring up at the ceiling. There was one remarkable mind churning inside this lovely cowgirl package.

Heaven help me, at that exact moment I fell in love with her.

## CHAPTER NINE

The next morning I drove past the graveyard, the park, and on into downtown Las Sombras, eager to begin work as designated researcher for the Ghost Hunters of Black Ash Canyon. Internet searches had revealed that the first and only newspaper in town was the *Las Sombras Tribune*, which began publishing in 1885 and was finally laid to rest in 1952. The municipal library possessed a full run. My vague plan was to skim the old issues for stories bearing on land surveys.

The town was already full of wannabe wine connoisseurs beginning a long day of sipping, considering, and passing judgment. Shy had suggested that I park in the front of the United Presbyterian Church, which maintained in its courtyard the nicest public bathrooms in the area. I found the place down a side street five blocks from the main drag. Its buildings sat on a half block, gracious but not grand. They were fronted by a broad lawn, deeply and uniformly green, several tall palm trees, and colorful flower beds. The chapel to the right was marked by a wooden cross and thick Romanesque doors. I walked into the courtyard next to the chapel. There appeared to be a rectory in the back of the property, but the stone-paved courtyard was enclosed by public buildings. Through a bank of large windows I saw a book-lined room where an adult education class of some sort was in session. There were benches in the courtyard and a wishing well. A picnic jug of ice water rested in the shade on a patio table next to a stack of paper cups. A few feet away was a copper basin full of clean water for dogs. I used the men's room. Nothing fancy, but of a piece with the delightful freshness of this entire institution. I made a mental note to thank Shy for the excellent tip.

My day at the Wilkerson Library began in disappointment. I hurried down to the basement stacks housing the *Las Sombras Tribune* only to learn that the early decades of the paper, through 1921, were missing.

The librarian was apologetic. Some years back heavy rains had flooded the basement, ruining the old *Tribunes*, which were not in good shape to begin with, and had been scheduled for microfilming. The staff had not yet found time to revise the internet catalogue. I looked around. The only staff in evidence was the middle-aged woman before me, and a slightly younger woman who was busy checking in DVDs. About half of the ground floor seemed to be given over to electronic media.

This seemed to be a common fate in the California library system. I had seen it during my early years in Paso Robles, and later in Los Angeles. Public libraries use their tax dollars to drive the old Mom and Pop video stores out of business.

I asked her if anyone had a full collection of the *Tribune*.

"I believe the *Las Sombras Sun* inherited the *Tribune's* own collection of its back issues. About a decade ago they leased the building that once housed the newspaper. It had been an art gallery for a while, then that folded, and eventually a developer redid the facades along the entire street. The *Sun* took out a lease on the original offices of the *Tribune*. Apparently a storeroom in the back contained the old paper's morgue, exactly as they had left it in 1952. The gallery owner hadn't wanted to throw the papers out and didn't need the space, so he just let it be."

"Does the *Sun* use it?"

"When they do historical pieces, yes, they tip in a few details from old *Tribune* material."

"But nothing anyone would call scholarship, assuming anyone knew what that was?"

The woman checking in the movies stifled a laugh.

"I shouldn't think so," the head librarian sniffily replied.

Following her directions, I went up a block to Statehood Boulevard, then two blocks to the right. The street, like much of Las Sombras, resembled an old frontier town, but made over for recent commercial interests, like a movie ranch or a country shopping mall. You walked on a wooden side-walk covered by an unbroken sequence of front porches, and spied the occasional mock hitching-post or what might once have been a horse trough repurposed as a planter for flower-ing vines. Meanwhile snatches of old Ennio Morricone scores echoed in your brain.

In front of the *Sun's* offices a young man with dark red hair, dressed in a T-shirt commemorating some rodeo, was loading bales of newspapers bound with plastic ties into the back door of a dusty black SUV. I tried the front door and found it locked.

I walked back to the young man. "Anyone in this morn-ing?"

He nodded. "My sister is. We went in through the back door. Knock loud. She's making coffee in the back."

I took his advice. Eventually Lorna Gonsalves, Shy's mo-tormouth friend I had met last Friday at the Stagecoach Bar & Grill, opened the door for me as her brother was pulling away, off to deliver free copies of the *Las Sombras Sun* to the stores and restaurants that were its major advertisers.

"Michael Buckman!" she exclaimed like a star struck teenager, pointing me to the most comfortable chair in the office/reception room and fetching me a cup of coffee. "You're just the man I've been wanting to see. That Cheyenne girl has gotten *terribly* secretive in recent years. Time was we told each other everything, but Friday at the Stagecoach she never mentioned that you were a famous author. *Adoration or Else* is the number nine bestseller in the non-fiction category according to Sunday's Los Angeles Times! You're news, Mike. I want to do a feature on you for the *Sun*."

My heart shriveled.

"Look, I came to this area in large part to escape publicity. I hope you'll respect that."

"I wasn't planning to ask about that ex-wife of yours. She's definitely in the running for Bitch of the Year."

"Right. And if she wins, I'm a shoe-in for Cuckold of the Year." I tried to change the subject. "I passed some words with your brother outside. He's the delivery boy?"

"You met Don? He's just beginning work this week. The poor boy has been at loose ends since he graduated from Auchincloss Prep. But he plans to attend Central Coast University in the spring. I was hoping that working for the *Sun* would give him some structure in the meantime. So why this visit, Mike?"

"I was just over at the town library. . . ." I had invented a pathetic story to hide my real interest in the *Las Sombras Tribune*. One of my AFI projects, so this piece of fiction went, was to determine whether the plots of silent westerns, especially those made by the American Film Manufacturing Company in La Mesa and later Santa Barbara, reflected real events in the early history of California. Hence my interest in older issues of the *Tribune*. A number of American's plots had involved the railroad, and I suspected that the early history of Las Sombras, being primarily a railroad town in those days, might prove useful.

Lorna was eager to help. She showed me the storage room containing open piles of old newspapers. "This isn't exactly museum-quality preservation," she remarked. "The older issues are often no more than one folded sheet printed on four sides. You have to be very careful with them. Even then some of them will break up in your hands. It's just the way the cookies crumble. Rain destroyed some of the library copies, but the generally dry climate around here will take all of them in the end." She set me up in a small office across from the archive.

But I wanted more from her, and was forced to tack on a second shoddy invention.

"Another thing you might help me with, Lorna. I've been hearing a lot about Dieter Thorson. A friend of mine in Los Angeles is working on a script about a serial killer in the California desert. I thought he might be able to use some elements of the Thorson case. I gather he left some note-books? Do you by any chance have copies of them?"

"You mean there might be a Thorson movie? That would be great! Sure, I have copies of those notebooks. I'm working on a piece linking the Thorson killings with the Vera Maarten murder. The female relatives of the Thorson victims have already contacted friends and relations of Vera Maarten. They're all getting together at the Stagecoach next Friday to do the *Cryin' Time* ritual. So I use these grieving women to tell the story of our first serial killings and their resumption with the Vera Maarten death. Good hook, don't you think? I'm calling it *Black Ash Canyon: Land of Dreams, Veil of Tears*. Some title, eh?"

After two prolonged falsehoods, a quick lie didn't seem like much. "That's a good one, Lorna. Classy."

"The 'land of dreams' comes from one of Dieter Thorson's notebooks. When he first sees Quicksilver Canyon, he calls it his 'land of dreams.' I think there's a good chance that the AP will pick up my piece. You know what that would mean, don't you? My byline in papers all over the world. This story could be my big break."

"Good luck with that."

She went back to the front office, pulled three slim volumes from a bookcase there, and handed them to me. The pages of the Thorson notebooks were zeroxed, and I supposed from their clear plastic covers that the books had been bound by a copy shop. I put them on the desk in my makeshift office. Lorna excused herself to do some errands, and I started in on the old *Tribunes*.

The piles were in roughly chronological order. The earliest issues were printed on a single sheet. I gathered that the first editor, Cyrus Gardner, had immigrated to California from upstate New York. He was well grounded in early American history. On the other hand, he was not a deeply imaginative or original man. There was a lot of puffery for the railroads—stories about the dignitaries, politicians, and celebrities who passed through the Las Sombras station. He was a great admirer of Lassiter Springs, and felt that the neighboring town had been founded on sounder principles than his own. Gardner lamented the lack of commercial ambition in Las Sombras, which he blamed on the debilitating effects of the Hartwell Tavern, a local saloon whose fisticuffs, knife fights, and occasional gun battles were reported with a studied vagueness. For some years there was a rumor that a Harvey House would be established in the Las Sombras depot. Gardner extolled the modern efficiency of a Harvey operation. A conductor would determine how many passengers would lunch in the dining room, how many at the counter, then wire this information ahead to the restaurant. But to  Gardner's chagrin, the Las Sombras Harvey House never happened.  He adamantly opposed the founding of New Aarhus, and in editorial after editorial lashed out at the follies of establishing a foreign city in an American state.

Gardner moved on or passed away, and a new editor-publisher, Samuel Balfour, took over the paper in 1895.  By that time the oil industry was moving into the area, and the larger ranchos, sequels to the gigantic ranches of the land-grant era, were being subdivided into ever smaller farms. Disparate people began settling in and around Las Sombras—squatters, miners, oil workers, small ranchers, various businessmen, a doctor, several lawyers, horse breeders, schoolmasters, pulmonary patients seeking relief in a hotter and drier climate, the occasional rich entrepreneur, and yes, an office of surveyors, J. T. Harding and Sons, who advertised that they had been trained at a school in San Francisco. Maybe California was after all (with no insult to Basin Street) America's land of dreams?  God knows its residents had often liked to think of themselves as custodians of a great spirituality variously related to climate and terrain.

Balfour looked with pleasure on these new signs of civilization.  He deplored saloons, opium smoking, and women of the night.  Like his predecessor, he found that the worst outrages to law and order occurred in or around Hartwell Tavern. I was reminded that decades later California would become one of the states most enthusiastically behind Prohibition.

I found a 1915 story about a murder on the outskirts of town allegedly committed by a fellow named "Four-Finger Jack" or "Bernardo Herrera." He was said to be a well-known ruffian from the San Francisco area, a famously quick-tempered man given to heavy drinking and sudden violence. In the immediate local case, the background of the violence was "wage disputes arising from a surveying project to the west of town." I perked up. West of the town included Black Ash Canyon! The victim was a man named Joseph Peckham, whose occupation was described as "chainman."

This looked promising. This looked very promising. I wrote down the names in the case, and checked subsequent issues for further references to the story. There was nothing until two weeks after the Peckham murder, when a deputy marshal, sent from Santa Barbara to "investigate recent crimes in this area," was found dead behind Hartwell's Tavern, shot three times in the back. I went through the next month of newspapers, but neither Mr. Herrera nor Mr. Peckham ever came up again. I wondered if the editor had feared for his life.

I decided to take a break from the *Tribune* and look at Dieter Thorson's journals.

They were of course sickening. The passage that had given Lorna Gonsalves her title proved to be the opening paragraph of the *Ghost Notebook*, describing Thorson's first look at Quicksilver Canyon:

> The place was all mine. There were turkey vultures in the air and on the ground lizards, gophers, squirrels, moles, jackrabbits. But no people in sight, not a one. It was my own land of dreams. I could really do good killing here.

It made me deeply queasy to read this appalling sentiment from an author doing his best to sound like the biblical Adam or one of those first explorers assessing the New World. Maybe Lorna had a good title at that.

Skimming ahead, I found a statement that Billy Steele had mentioned to the Ghost Killers. Thorson was talking about his spirit guide. "He is the chainman, he knows where the boundaries are. He has other names too. He is the master, he is the inchworm of death." I copied this puzzling information into my own notebook.

"And who," came a voice from the doorway, "are you, may I ask?"

A balding man with a bushy mustache was standing in the doorway. I had been too intent on my research to register his entrance.

I explained that Lorna Gonsalves had given me free run of the back office and storage room. He introduced himself as Jim Freeman, the film critic of the *Las Sombras Sun*. Since there was no movie theatre in Las Sombras, he spent his time hopping from one neighboring city to another, to as far north as San Luis Obispo and as far south as Santa Barbara. He was just now returning from matinees in a Santa Maria cineplex, where he had managed to see three features and enough of a fourth to be set for the next two issues of the *Sun*. "I thought I wanted to sell insurance," he told me, "but I didn't. This is the best job I've ever had, save for the pay. All I have to do is sound off about a couple of movies every other week."

"Tell me, Jim. Who is the main expert around here on local history?" Every town had at least one. A interview with a keen amateur historian might save me some library work.

"Well, there's a guy who runs a fruit stand between here and New Aarhus, Mason Brooks, who knows a lot about the movie history of the area. He wrote a book on the American Film Company's work in Santa Barbara. But for the general history of these parts you can't do better than Byron Kinsolving.  He teaches at the Auchincloss Academy, which owns a big stretch of land to the east of town."

I got directions, fetched the truck, and found my way down a poplar-lined private driveway to a gate house manned by a pleasant fellow in a pseudo-ranger outfit with a patch on his chest reading "Auchincloss Preparatory School, Est. 1951."  He asked me my business.  I told him that I wanted to see Byron Kinsolving.  He consulted a clipboard.  Mr. Kinsolving was holding office hours now.  But he would be finished in half an hour, if I cared to wait.  He gave me a brochure with a map, pointed out Kinsolving's building, and waved me in.

I found the office and took a seat in the waiting area.  Two boys were also sitting there.  One of them was a wiry fellow with black hair whose sweatshirt pictured a grimacing singer beneath the words "Wild Child"—the name, I assumed, of some modern rockers.  The other, younger-looking boy wore gym shorts and a hoody with a ziggurat structure on the front, inscribed with hieroglyphs I took to be of Aztec origin.  I tried to strike up a conversation, but they were both stingy with words, and seemed to be saving their thoughts for Mr. Kinsolving.

A girl left the office.  From within we heard a spirited "Next!"  The wild child guy entered and closed the door.  I again tried conversation with Aztec Boy, and this time, all alone with me, he opened up. His name was Pete Larson. Along with five other students, he was taking an independent study with Mr. Kinsolving in survivalism.

"Making fires, getting clean water, which mushrooms to eat, that sort of thing?"

"Yeah. We're preparing for a three-day camping trip in the hills on the eastern tip of the campus. This unit has a great reputation with students. On the camping trip everyone stays up late while Mr. Kinsolving tells ghost stories."

"Do you like ghost stories?"

"My dad has a collection of Stephen King and Charles Grant books. I've read a few. I liked them pretty much."

We talked about supernatural fiction for a bit.

"So what's the book on Mr. Kinsolving? Is he easy to work with?"

"Sure, yeah. I guess he appeals more to nerds than jocks. Some of the seniors call him Kinsolving the Caring because he always sympathizes with misfits and loners."

"Kinsolving the Caring? Like the stock epithet of an Anglo-Saxon king?"

He nodded. I reflected that the students at Auchincloss Prep were getting an impressive education. I doubted whether Common Core had time for royal epithets.

Soon the door opened again. Wild Child hit the road and Pete Larson scooted into the inner sanctum. When he finally left, a tall man with long blond-grey hair and a trimmed beard strolled into the waiting area. He wore khaki pants with lots of pockets and a blue work shirt with rolled-up sleeves displaying muscular forearms.

"You must be Mike Buckman. George"—the name of the gate house guard—"called me about you. I'm Byron Kinsolving. Come on in."

Inside was the standard office decoration in the teaching trade—shelves of books. To one side of Kinsolving's desk was a display of Native American beadwork, a bow, and a leather quiver with some arrows in it.

I saw no advantage in concealing my mission entirely.

"I'm told that you're an able local historian. I was looking through early issues of the *Las Sombras Tribune* today, and found a story about a man named Herrera who might have murdered a certain Joseph Peckham in 1915. According to Samuel Balfour, the crime originated in a wage dispute over a surveying project to the west of town. Do you know anything about this incident?"

Kinsolving thought for a moment. "No, I don't. Of course Sam Balfour, like Gardner before him, was a terrible prig. All evil stemmed from Hartwell Tavern."

"I suppose they were easterners originally?"

He smiled. "To the core. Both of them came to California because they read a little book called *California for the Traveler and Health Seeker.* The railroad had commissioned a journalist named Charles Nordhoff to write a pamphlet pushing the health benefits of the California climate around Santa Barbara. He was, by the way, the grandfather of the Charles Nordhoff who later co-authored *Mutiny on the Bounty.* Both Gardner and Balfour were sickly men whose health improved in the California climate, but they couldn't abide the frontier lawlessness of the state, and yearned for it to hurry up and become easternized."

"Are there any books about the history of surveying in the state?"

"Well, almost any key topic gets treated somewhere in the thirty-nine volumes of Hubert Bancroft. But that's not really my field. I've concentrated on the industries of mining, railroading, and oil exploration."

"They all involve surveying."

"Peripherally, yes. What doesn't?"

"I'm interested in the criminal sides of surveying."

"Well, I know that ever since statehood in 1851 there have been scams and schemes involving that profession, some of them reaching all the way to the California Surveyor

General's office.  The big ranchos had to be surveyed before they were ratified by the United States.  Later on there was a similar process with  towns and cities, ports, roads, mines, oil fields, and so on.  You don't get civilization until boundaries and passages are precisely defined.  Fraud and corruption dogged the whole process.  They always seem to come along for the ride."

"Could you recommend some books on late nineteenth-century outlaws in California?"

"That's a thriving field, actually.  When non-professionals read California history, most of them gravitate to lawbreakers, gun play, old atrocities.  Matt Chambers has made good money satisfying that need.  He's accurate.  He writes well. There are lots of Chambers books with similar titles— *California Bandits*, *California Outlaws*, *Villains of Old California*, and so on—and they all have the same format.  One chapter for each outlaw.  Chambers shapes a biography, using other historians, newspaper stories, military records, and small library archives.  He's the best place to start, and he may also be the best place to end."

We talked about local history resources.  There was a Historical Society in New Aarhus, though its primary interest was in the cultural and familial links between its oldest families and Denmark.  An annual Depot Days pageant was staged in Las Sombras. The Pageant Committee boasted residents with a keen passion for historical matters. A similar event in Lassiter Springs, the yearly Harvest Festival in October, involved a sizeable display of old farming technology.

"I met an Auchincloss graduate today. Don Gonsalves? He's the new delivery boy at the *Las Sombras Sun*."

"I know him. He plans to enter Central Coast College this spring."

"I understand Dieter Thorson was a student here."

Kinsolving's expression stiffened. "You're interested in Thorson?"

Here I thought it best to hide my cards.

"People are talking about him lately, what with the Vera Maarten murder last week. Did you know him by any chance? Did you teach him?"

"He took my course in California history. Average grade. Then he signed up for an independent study with me, but I didn't see much of him that semester. No school can be proud of all of its graduates. Dieter struck most of us at Auchincloss as a weak student and a normal person. He had girlfriends, he seemed to be social enough. Obviously there were terrible places inside the boy, but no one at the Academy realized that until after his crimes."

Kinsolving the Caring had not given much care to Dieter Thorson. He seemed well-adjusted, with girlfriends and social skills.

I saw through the back window that afternoon light was rapidly thinning out. I wanted to check something before the library closed, so I said my goodbyes to Byron Kinsolving and drove back to town, parking next to the library. I used one of their computers to punch up my desktop screen at AFI. A perk of working there was access to the online *Oxford English Dictionary.* I opened the program, entered my password, and looked up several entries.

Jackpot! According to this venerable authority on English words, *inchworm* was an old slang term for a surveyor. It must have to do with the insect's peculiar locomotion. It draws itself up until the front part touches the back, then the front moves forward and the back gradually draws up again. Similarly, a surveyor extends his chain, then the back end catches up with the front, and the front is extended again. The word *caterpillar*—presumably for the same reason— could also name a surveyor. There was even a specific caterpillar that seventeenth-century Englishmen called "the surveyor."

As Billy had explained, being a *chainman* was a menial job. It didn't take any special training to extend the chain to the next position and secure it with an arrow. But our master ghost had worked his way to the top of the ladder. He had become an inchworm, a full-fledged surveyor.

The library was closing. I drove to the Presbyterian Church and parked. Then I walked back into town and decided to have dinner at a clean well-lighted place called the Oak Barrel Cafe. While I ate, I gathered my thoughts. I knew the master ghost had spent his life surveying California, probably as a chainman early in life, then later as a bonafide surveyor. I had a line on one surveyor, Herrera, who had perhaps committed a murder in this part of California in 1915. The next thing to do was to check through the books of Matt Chambers, looking for a chapter on Herrera or another criminal surveyor from the period. I was close.

I also wanted to know more about Byron Kinsolving. His very name exuded suspicion. He had taught Dieter Thorson. And King Kinsolving the Caring told ghost stories.

I took my time, had a couple glasses of wine and a slice of olallieberry pie for dessert. It was dark outside when I left the restaurant.

I turned down the side street that led to the church. In the first block I heard the wine-bar piano and soft conversation spilling onto the sidewalk from The Court Jester, a restaurant I had considered and rejected. The second block was quieter. From Peter's Upscale Corral came the clatter of plates being cleared away. On the outer edge of the business district, with the sounds of business being done faint behind me, I walked by a boarded-up video store and a public bulletin board.

I was now in a residential area, and the silence immediately deepened. In these energy-conscious times, only a few porch lights were burning. I saw the flickering colors of a television through a crack in drawn curtains, heard the muted surge of a sitcom laugh track. Half a moon shed enough light to cast shadows. Dark bushes and trees were leaving oily impressions of themselves on the ground. I zipped up my jacket. It was cold.

Two blocks ahead lights shone from the church courtyard. I heard footsteps behind me.

I stopped. The footsteps stopped. I made a quarter turn and looked back. A half block behind me was a circle of light. As a cigarette got lit, I glimpsed a dark-haired male face. I straightened and walked on. Within seconds the footsteps resumed.

There was no good reason to dread these steps. But they spooked me a little, tapping away behind me at my own exact pace, like a clock marking for some unknown purpose my consumption of time. I struggled to put the right word on my emotion. I felt . . . *surveyed*. That feeling was back. Reason called for calm. But a shudder of dread accompanied the reappearance in my mind of the word *surveyed*.

Reason continued to counsel me. I was within earshot of downtown Las Sombras. I was on my way to a church. There was one guy behind me. I was a large man in the prime of life. If need be, I could take care of myself.

I saw my truck parked in front of the well-lit church. I walked to it, tossed my notebook on the passenger seat. I could no longer hear footsteps. They had gone in a direction different from mine.

I could drive home, but I preferred to empty my bladder first. I walked down the wide stone path joining the sidewalk to the church courtyard. I entered the men's room, flipping an illuminated switch next to the door. Light sprang into the pleasant, fresh-smelling bathroom.

I did my business at the urinal. I washed my hands. I checked my image in the mirror and smiled at its apparent calm and normality.

With an abrupt pop the lights went out. Footsteps approached the door and stopped. The door opened. A dark male form stood silhouetted against the courtyard lights. A smoky mass shot toward me, as before in Old Cabin, and again I was roughly elbowed aside on the throne of my self-consciousness.

I waited. The invader took his time. Then I heard my inner voice. It was the same inner voice to which I had listened all my life. But it was not me speaking.

*Something new.*

I answered the inner voice that was not mine with the inner voice that was. *What do you mean?*

I was being painfully stupid in this pretense of ignorance, for I had seen the memories he had been examining and knew exactly what he meant.

*Why do you ask? We both see that you are sweet on Cheyenne Griswold.*

*Yes.*

*What you know of me is accurate. I invade minds. I control them. I cannot be killed.*

My response was born of terror and frivolity. *Not even by a nuclear bomb?*

*You are trying to frighten me. Boo! Ha ha.*

Having my own scornful laugh aimed at me was enraging. I was suddenly insane with anger. *You can be frightened! How about that putrid pit in the back of the quicksilver mine? Take a dive in that, you bastard! You're a miserable thing. You can't enjoy a real life. Your only aim is to ruin real lives.*

I ranted on, heaping obscenities on top of insults. I knew, as I mounted this futile tirade, that words would never hurt this being. He stopped me with a simple command. I think now that I was unconsciously waiting for it. *You must stop tracking me down, Michael.*

*And if I don't?* I was being stupid again. I knew a threat was coming. I knew what the threat was. Defiantly, madly, I wanted to hear him say it. He was a surveyor, wasn't he? I wanted to see the boundary.

*And if you don't, I will take Cheyenne out of this world. There is no other. Cross me, and you'll never ever know her again.*

I wanted to hide my thinking from him, but I couldn't. There was no difference between thinking and the inner voice. *If you could kill her, why don't you just kill me? I don't believe you.*

*I could in time break you down, master you, enslave you. But Cheyenne? Presto! And it is done. Think what I have accomplished with her mother.*

I tried to think of nothing.

*That frightens you. How wise! If you do not stop tracking me, I will take Cheyenne away.*

The next thing I knew the lights buzzed back on. I was staring at myself in the mirror. I looked frightened, small, pathetic. As before, I felt defiled, had the same hung-over sense of being dirty and ashamed. But at Old Cabin there had been no messages from the invader. This time I was overwhelmed by a sense of helplessness. He could not die. Words would never hurt him. I knew of nothing that would hurt him.

I was in the grip of another emotion, compounded of loneliness, exhaustion, and relief. The door had closed on a disturbing visitor. For now he was gone. This weave of feelings, compared to the sense of powerlessness, felt like hope. I was on my own. He was too busy to take me over, and forced to rely on threats. That gave me a margin of freedom. Maybe not much, maybe not for long, but enough to give me a chance. I would keep on researching him. The very fact that he had warned me to stop suggested I must be on the right track. Somehow I would discover a vulnerability, find a possible weapon.

Billy Steele thought this a uniquely powerful and vicious spirit. He might one day soon take control of Shy. He might possess her even if I beat back my deepest instincts and quit tracking him down. The best way to protect the woman I loved, likely the only way, was to kill him.

I returned to Shady Grove Cabin and had just poured myself a scotch when Shy appeared at the door. She asked about my day. Though I hadn't decided for sure, my instincts were to keep the Inchworm's threat to myself. I saw no benefit in alarming Cheyenne. Shy might already be in mortal danger. I didn't want to stir that pot by letting the ghost know that I had disobeyed his command, for which the announced punishment was the loss of Cheyenne. But this plan would force me to misrepresent, fib, and withhold. Even if I could convince Shy to back off and leave Valentina be for a while, she would continue to see her mother. I had to assume that, if she knew about my researches, Shy might somehow betray this knowledge to her mother, and therefore to the ghost inhabiting her. The Inchworm might even slip into Shy's mind and take a look for himself.

So I took a first step into the mire of misrepresentation, answering her question with an evasive remark about organizing my research plans. She did not probe my reply because the story of her own hair-raising day was yearning to be told.

That afternoon Shy and her mother renewed a ritual they had enjoyed together almost as far back as her memory stretched. It was the great game of mother handing down to daughter. The ritual began with the two of them systematically looking through Valentina's closets. Shy would express her admiration for this or that item, a scarf or a sweater coat, things once much admired but now rarely if ever worn. Valentina would then pass on to her daughter the admired pieces. They moved along, still playing Hand-Me-Down, to her mother's jewelry boxes.

When they were done with those, Valentina climbed up on a step stool and reached into the back corner of a top shelf, from which she withdrew a small pile of old sketchbooks and diaries dating from her childhood. Cheyenne had never seen them before. Even in the best of times, she had been aware that her mother was withdrawn, secretive in fact, keeping a side of herself entirely hidden from the world. Valentina gripped the stack of old books in her lap, refusing to allow her daughter to touch them. She opened the top one, a sketchbook, and slowly turned the pages while Cheyenne gazed down from over her shoulder.

The drawings began depicting the same things that surrounded her today: mountains, cliffs, streams, trees, horses, barns, cabins. Near the middle of the book was a drawing of a male. Valentina paused over it. On the left side of the page was a child's usual rendering of the sun, a circle surrounded by spokes of light rays. On the other side, the man had been given a flamboyantly outsized moustache. His head of hair was rendered with great care. Careful strokes, mirroring each other and almost touching each other, indicated the impression his wavy locks had made on the young Valentina. Above his head the child had drawn a scimitar of moon.

"*Mi rey plateado*," Valentino said. Hispanic through her mother's lineage, Cheyenne knew the Spanish language, though she read it better than she spoke it. *Mi rey plateado*, she thought to herself, "my silver king." Her father worked with silver in his saddlery. Could it be him?

Before she could ask about the silver-haired figure, Valentina turned the page. Now she beheld a drawing of two figures that the child had for some reason turned against. The figures were heavily scribbled over. Again she turned the page. Two people were lying on a cot. Devil's horns sprouted from their foreheads. The page turned once more. A little girl was standing before a building with a burning twig in her hand, about to light a brush pile on fire. One could see right through the walls of the building, which looked to be a barn. Inside were the two adults from the previous page, again with horns, but now they were lying on the same bed. New page. The barn was in flames. An angel with a halo hovered above it, his hair carefully rendered. It was the *rey plateado* in a divine form. New page. Shy saw with horror the sketch of a girl standing in the devastated barn, a pile of black ashes where the beds and their occupants had been. Above these remains the silver angel floated, blessing the scene.

"Who was your silver king, mother? It wasn't Angel, was it?"

Valentina looked up at her for an instant, shaking her head. "Certainly not. He was the true angel, not father. Father and mother are burning in hell." She went back to her sketches.

"Tell me, mom. Who was the silver king?"

"Be patient, Cheyenne. I'm sure you will meet him. There's a ghost in the cellar, sweetheart. Look for him. It won't be long now." She slowly turned her face toward Cheyenne, her eyes gleaming and her mouth fixed in a grin so wicked and rigid that her daughter recoiled. "I'm sure he will have *something special* for you."

It all came together in my mind with a surge of ice-cold dread. Valentina was too exposed, too obviously the ghost's receptacle. She had served him well. As a child she had lit the barn on fire and burned her parents to death. As an old woman she had burned their ghosts out of Old Cabin. But now the time of her usefulness had almost expired. Valentina was a frail old woman, at the end of her days. There could be little doubt as to where the spirit's new home would be. The mother had been a comfortable haunt. The daughter would be too. I had been terrorized by a meaningless threat. For whether I ceased researching him or not, he meant to possess Cheyenne. He must have been planning it for years now, perhaps from the moment Shy was born.

Only a small window of hope was left to me. By keeping my researches secret, I might buy some time.

"She wasn't just passing on her clothes and jewels, Shy. She was passing on the ghost. Whatever Billy recommended, you have to stay away from her for the time being."

She nodded. "But it wasn't her, Mike! I knew for certain it was the ghost inside her speaking to me."

How right I had been! I opened my arms and she fell sobbing against my chest.

CHAPTER TEN

The next morning I had a plan. It wasn't brilliant or elaborate, but it would prevent Shy from learning about my activities and inadvertently passing them on to the Inchworm. First of all, I had to get out of Black Ash Canyon. The burden of seeing Cheyenne every day and lying to her about my activities would be too much of a strain for me to handle.

I told Shy that, for reasons of efficiency, I was going to spend the next few days in Las Sombras. I would be scooting around from library to library, perhaps interviewing historians, and it seemed best to operate from a base in town.

"I assume you have leads," she said, inviting me to confide in her.

"Sure I do," I replied, then took some giant steps into the badlands of fibbing and evasion. "But I've always been superstitious about research assumptions. I don't like to talk about them until they really pan out. And remember what I said last night about your mother, Shy. I would let her be at this point. I think the rest of her story is waiting out there in books and papers. I'll find out everything we need." We kissed goodbye.

I was stowing my suitcase and laptop in the truck when I saw Solly's Land Rover headed for the main gate. I waved and strolled toward him. He turned my way. His window snicked down.

"I'm heading for Steele's place to discuss ghost weapons. Care to join us?"

"I'll be right behind you."


"Our first idea," Billy said, dressed today in a black T shirt and an antique bomber jacket his grandfather had worn in World War II, "was to weaponize salt and iron by loading them into 12-guage shotgun shells. It's been tried before. Some paranormalists claim that the results have been spectacularly positive in the sense that the doctored ammo makes ghostly targets change position. They move, they retreat when peppered with little squadrons of streaking salt and iron bits. I have my doubts. But you *can* see and hear ghosts, and they have some control over the physical world. To do that, in my view, they have to have some physical substrate of their own—be it the old standby 'ectoplasm' or some newer name for the same thing. And if they are physical in some fashion, they can be affected by physical weapons of some fashion."

Certain that his prey had been trained in nineteenth-century surveying, Billy was going to attack him with iron from period correct instruments. He had purchased an antique Gunter chain from EBay, thirty-three feet of iron links with two poles and a group of ten iron arrows. It was due to arrive tomorrow. He had already broken down the arrow we found in Outlaw Creek into filings for his shotgun shells.

"Ghost ammunition. . . . Is that all we have?" I asked, unimpressed. Assuming we encountered the ghost indoors or in a mine, shotgun blasts might be more of a danger than an advantage.

Bill shrugged. "Solly had a rather grand idea the other day, but I fear it's wholly impractical."

"Tell me about it," I said, turning to my older teammate.

As Solly presented the idea, I became progressively more excited. It was at the very least a notable case of overkill, a tactic beyond the imagination of our unspeakable villain. I liked that. "But for one thing," he finished, "Billy is right. The cost is prohibitive."

"How long would it take?"

"If we started tomorrow, maybe a week."

"And how much would it cost?"

Solly, doing the math, pursed his lips and bobbed his head. "Say, upwards of half a million for the basic structure. Another million would have to be set aside to pay the likely fines from the State of California."

"Get started, this afternoon if possible. I'll pay."

They began pleading that I really shouldn't do such an outlandish thing, that I ought to reconsider, that it might not work and all my money would go to waste.

I waved them off. "Believe me, I can afford it. You may have heard about my recent divorce? Set up a bank account, Solly, and I'll transfer the money." I let them know where I would be residing for the next few days.

"And for another thing," Billy cautioned, "we still need to figure out how to capture the Chainman."

"We have a week to do that. Let's all of us concentrate on that problem, and forget about the shotguns. I have some good research leads. Maybe a fuller knowledge of the ghost will point us toward a solution."

I rented a room in the nicest hotel in the area, the Green Pastures Inn and Day Spa on a country road between Las Sombras and New Aarhus. The hotel was owned and managed by a Central Coast potentate named Baron Samson, a former actor from Virginia who had starred in many success-ful martial arts action flicks. He was known to his detractors, who were legion, as The Ham from Harrisonburg, though he much preferred to be called The Kicks from Styx. Thirty years ago he had left Hollywood behind and invested in a large vineyard in the Santa Ynez Valley. Prospering, he branched out into local real estate ventures and soon opened the Green Pastures.

In recent days I had scoped out the hotel from the road. The parking lot was hidden behind the complex's major structure, a useful feature for someone who didn't want to call attention to himself. Before registering, I took a good long look around the lobby. It was a large room centered on an imposing stone fireplace, with lots of nooks and snugs. There were two restaurants, one for breakfast and lunch and another for dinner. I also located a handful of discrete but alert-seeming security personnel whose duty was to watch over the wealthy guests, some of whom were celebrities. The Green Pastures gave every sign of being the safest and most discrete place for me to stay. I requested and received a corner room.

Once settled, I signed into the hotel's Wi-Fi system and checked the internet for copies of Thorson's notebooks. There were sites all over the world, in Scandinavia, Eastern

Europe, Indonesia, and South Africa, on which the three notebooks still resided, as safely as specimens in a vault, to be read, downloaded, and printed.

I called a friend of mine in Los Angeles, Pat Dworkin, known in his early hacking career as "Magic Dork" or "Wizard Fingers." These days he was in the business of designing and maintaining computer networks, including the system at the American Film Institute. If anyone could help me out, it was Pat.

I outlined the problem. Thorson's three notebooks had been posted on the internet soon after his death in 1993. The documents were still available. Was there any way at this point of determining who had posted them?

"Here's what probably happened," Pat began. "The documents were sent to an anonymity server. He removed the header from the files, so that no one could tell where they originated, and sent them to his worldwide network of free-speech websites. They posted them. Generally speaking, threats from law enforcement or intelligence agencies don't work with these free-speech anonymity sites. They're true believers. They aren't phased by the argument that anonymity posting protects con artists, drug dealers, kidnappers, pedophiles, libelers, hatespeakers, traitors, and terrorists. They expect pressure, and they are prepared to resist it."

"But there are still ways to trace the postings?"

"Well, I can find out the name of the anonymity poster to whom the documents were originally sent. He is the only one who would have a record of their source."

"Do charge me for this service."

"Be happy to."

I gave him my cell number.

I spent the next three days collecting from local libraries and reading the Matt Chambers books recommended to me by Byron Kinsolving. As I had been warned, they bore confusingly similar titles such as *Frontier Outlaws: The Criminals of Early California* and *Renegades and Scalawags: Tales of California Outlaws*. They contained neither bibliographies nor indexes, though their chapters were sparsely footnoted. I skimmed them all, becoming familiar with the exploits of Black Bart, Joaquin Murrieta, Tiburcio Vasquez, English Jim, and numerous other thieves and killers plaguing California in the nineteenth century. I found incidental allusions to surveying scams, but nothing detailed and no footnoted sources worthy pursuit.

At the end of those three frustrating days, I was sitting in the Green Pastures dining room waiting for a meal of crab cakes when a tall man with sparse hair approached my table. He wore a leather coat and a diamond cross hung from his neck on a thick gold chain.

He pointed to the book at my side. "I see you're reading Matt Chambers. Mind if I sit down for a minute? I'm Baron Samson."

"I thought I recognized you. Have a seat."

In response to Samson's questions about my interest in Chambers' works, I told him that I was researching old murders related to the profession of surveying, particularly the death of Joseph Peckham, a boy who might have been killed by a surveyor named Herrera.

"Don't know about that one. But I did write a book about murderers in the early years of California statehood. Called it *Gunslingers and Bar Brawlers*. I know that sounds like a Chambers title, but I think I was a little more honest than he is about what we know and what we like to suppose. Have you noticed that everything in Chambers sounds like a movie description?"

Samson was right. There weren't any gaps or guesses in the stories of Matt Chambers. They were suspiciously shapely, exactly like movie plots.

"Did you run across anything about surveyors or falsified surveys?"

"Not in my research, no. But anyone who has owned and sold as much California land as I have becomes familiar with false surveys. Back in the old days everyone wanted to lay claim to more land than they actually owned. You hired a surveyor and bribed him to expand your boundaries, or what is the same thing, shrink your neighbor's boundaries. That fear helped to create the title insurance racket, which was one of the most successful con games in American history."

"When was this?"

"End of the nineteenth, start of the twentieth century."

"I haven't learned much from Chambers, and what I did learn I'm not sure I trust."

"Why read him at all?"

"A teacher at the Auchincloss Academy recommended him."

"Must have been Kinsolving."

I nodded. "The same."

He snorted. "Sonofabitch gave me a snotty review in one of the Los Angeles papers. Said that in my search for authenticity I 'lost sight of the romanticism of the era.' Romanticism! In gold rush California? Give me a break. All those greedy bastards, half of them deserters and wanted criminals, gone stark raving mad with gold fever, jumping each other's claims, buying off their neighbors' employees, forming vigilante gangs to murder innocent men, and so on." He let himself calm down for a few seconds. "Why the surveying angle?"

"It figures prominently in one of Dieter Thorson's journals, *The Ghost Notebook*. You remember him? The serial killer? He seems to have been in touch with the spirit of a criminal surveyor he calls 'The Inchworm.' That's an old slang term for a surveyor."

"You know, I met Thorson once in 1992. My book had come out in 1990, and he wanted to ask me questions about the early lives of some of my outlaws. Or so he claimed. Turned out that he had watched a whole slew of my movies, and wanted to know about how to kill people with your hands and feet. *Death Punch* and *Death Grip* made a particularly big impression on him. Are you a movie fan?"

"Yeah. I've seen those movies."

"OK. Well, this Thorson guy thought there really *were* secret death punches and death grips. He wanted me to tell him how they were done."

Before Thorson debated between killing with a gun and killing with a knife, he had apparently considered the possibility of using his own body. Nothing like an enquiring young mind.

"What did he want to know about the outlaws?"

"Near as I can remember, he had a short list of questions. Did they live alone? Did they have any schooling? Did they live to be old and famous, and did young killers look them up for advice?"

"Like in the movies."

"Yeah. I tried to tell him that he was romanticizing those old fuckups."

The next day I drove to the Hans Christian Andersen Library in New Aarhus, where they had the only copy around of Baron Samson's *Gunslingers and Bar Brawlers*. I looked for the book in the stacks, but in the end I never got there. I was on my way to its call number when my attention was drawn to a yellow volume with black stamping. The author, King Harkins, had titled his gaudy book *Cheap Life: Killers of Old California*. This one had not popped up in my internet research. Neither Kinsolving nor Samson had mentioned it. I pulled the book down, flipped through. Again no index or bibliography, but just footnotes after each chapter, as in the Chambers books. But this time none of that mattered. All I needed was a glance at the table of contents: Chapter Two was called "Bernardino Herrera, Satan's Surveyor."

I took the volume back to my table, pulses drumming with anticipation. I was not disappointed. That you may judge my satisfaction for yourself, here is the meat of its Herrera chapter:

Bernardino was the bastard son of Octavio Herrera, a Spanish Captain who served the Mexican administration of California in various capacities in the Monterey and San Francisco area. Nothing is known of the mother, though in his correspondence Octavio makes it clear that he had no interest whatsoever in marrying her. She was "low" and came from "a poor family of no account." Yet he apparently felt some responsibility toward his offspring. In 1850, before leaving the new State of California for a diplomatic post in Mexico City, he arranged for the ten-year-old child to be apprenticed to a surveying firm in San Francisco. The company sent a crew, including Bernardino, to survey a ranch in a rocky corner of Sonoma County.

Apparently the boy riled other members of the team by insisting that there was only "one way" to do a proper survey, and that was with a Gunter chain. The crew was still using the old Spanish method of the *reata*, where measurements were done on horseback using a rawhide rope that tended over time to stretch out from its initially fixed length, leading to inaccuracies in a surveyor's measurements. The older employees, resenting the boy's arrogance, decided to teach the newcomer a lesson.

They walked him to the edge of a steep ravine, then formed a semi-circle around him. When young Herrera tried to leave, the boys linked arms like a human chain and refused him passage. There was only "one way," they informed Bernardino, to leave the cliff. Hours later the lad was hungry, exhausted, and terrified, not to mention sorely in need of relieving himself. His tormentors were correct. There was only one way out. Herrera jumped, tumbling over rocks and sharp bushes until a clump of boulders halted his downward course. He was covered with cuts and bruises. The rock that had possibly saved his life also smashed his left hand.

Herrera lost his index finger, gaining the nickname of "Four-Fingered Jack." Like a number of the period's outlaws, Herrera by the end of his career had a whole pack of sonorous nicknames. He was also the Inchworm of Death, Satan's Surveyor, Hell's Bench Mark, the Chainman of Doom.

Bad hand and all, the boy resumed his chain-man's duties within a week. A month later a mysterious campsite fire resulted in the deaths of two young men on the team. Young Herrera claimed innocence, though the team's senior surveyors felt certain that he had been responsible. He was not charged.

In the years to come his wayward deeds left deposits of lurid material in newspapers throughout California. He killed two men in a saloon knife fight. He began an adulterous affair with the wife of a rich farmer he intended to rob. His plans went awry when the farmer attacked him with a rifle. Herrera killed the man with his pistol, plundered his savings and belongings, burned his farm, and absconded with his wife. Two months later she was found dead at the foot of a cliff in Calaveras County. He was accused of a payroll robbery in the gold rush town of Angel's Camp. He assaulted and almost killed a policeman in another saloon brawl in Monterey.

In 1858 he was sentenced to five years in San Quentin for stealing horses. He escaped in the major prison break of June, 1859, but was recaptured a year later after having been arrested for a surveying fraud. He was returned to San Quentin and placed in heavy irons. But six months later Governor Leland Stanford granted him a clemency pardon because he was believed to have contracted consumption. Upon release, however, the prisoner's bloody cough mysteriously dried up. Herrera was once again free to pursue his wayward path through life.

There were other crimes, large and small: murders for which he was accused but never convicted, robberies that never stuck, fights over women and gambling debts. His next jail term arose from a relatively minor incident in San Francisco in 1884. Herrera was caught stealing a book on modern surveying instruments from H. H. Bancroft & Co.'s massive bookstore on Market Street in San Francisco.

The owner, of course, was the great historian of the Pacific coast, Hubert Howe Bancroft. He had amassed a stupendous private library, eventually running to 60,000 volumes, related to the history of the region. In 1884 he was, aided by a team of hired researchers, firmly embarked on the Herculean task of historiography that would by the end produce thirty-nine weighty volumes. Bancroft might not have prosecuted the thief, but police found over forty more books stolen from his store among Herrera's possessions. The thief had apparently been spending his afternoons for the last month browsing in the sizeable bookstore and stealing, day after day, a volume or two at a time. The historian-owner did prosecute, and brought his considerable influence to bear on making sure that Herrera's peccadillo was punished to the full extent of the law. Even though the books had been recovered, Herrera was sentenced to a year in jail. Insubordination and fighting with other inmates again landed our intemperate anti-hero in heavy chains. But let us not forget that this man delighted in chains. He used the iron links binding his hands to strangle a fellow inmate, and was sentenced to another ten years for manslaughter. Luckily for Bernardino, criminal associates arranged a successful jailbreak for him in 1887.

In that same year, soon after Herrera had been freed, Bancroft's eight-story building on Market Street burned to the ground. A fire in the basement of an adjacent Chinese laundry was officially blamed for the disaster. But persistent rumors at the time identified Herrera as the man responsible for the laundry fire. Given the Inchworm of Death's penchant for burning enemies, evident from his very first job in the surveying field, and given his extraordinary vengefulness, the rumors may well have been true.

In one of history's fascinating little twists, there is a footnote in a Bancroft volume on California reflecting on a 1861 atrocity in Alameda County. Four white settlers were waylaid after buying some supplies from a Spanish rancho. Mexican ranch hands were blamed for the crime. Though they were never convicted, most local residents believed that these men had set out after the white customers, hoping to settle political and racial scores. But the puzzling element of the crime was its unprecedented ferocity. The victims were bound, then stoned and mutilated. "One man," Bancroft wrote, "had had his lower jaw broken off and torn from his face with a reata, a noose-rope used to capture animals."

The historian cannot believe that such an outrage was committed by the peaceful Mexican ranch hands of that place and time. He goes on to suggest that the crime was actually committed by a couple of nomadic banditos, Juan Padilla and Ramon Ramirez, aided by a younger cutthroat named "Four-Fingered

Jack." Bancroft seems not to have connected this young psychopath with the man who robbed him of forty volumes on mathematical instruments for measuring topography, and who may later have unleashed his latent ferocity in razing Mr. Bancroft's tower of books. A reata, we should remember, was the Mexican-Spanish precursor of the chain. Bernardino Herrera had as a boy asked his first surveying team to replace their reata with a chain. This weapon would have appealed to the highwayman known as the Chainman of Doom.

After the Bancroft fire he drifted south, no doubt working under various aliases. He was probably the "Bernardo Haredo" who captained numerous surveying teams under the so-called Benson Syndicate, which exploited the federal government's Special Deposit System to defraud the citizenry of millions of dollars and the western states of countless acres of public land. He was almost certainly the "Four-Fingered Jack Herrado" who burned a waterfront hotel to the ground in Santa Barbara in 1891. By 1895 he discovered the title insurance business under the name "Bernard Hurdado," providing dummy surveys to go with invented title searches.

In 1915 he must have felt that his criminal past in the San Francisco area was safely behind him, for we find Satan's Surveyor working under his own name, Bernardino Herrera, in the northern part of Santa Barbara County. He seems to have murdered a fellow worker in what was said to be a disagreement over wages. The victim, a thirteen-year-old chainman from San Diego named Joe Peckham, was found strangled to death outside the city of Las Sombras, a chain still wrapped around his neck. A Sheriff's deputy was dispatched from Santa Barbara to investigate the killing. The deputy was found shot three times from behind outside Hartwell's Tavern, a notoriously rough saloon in Las Sombras. The local newspaper ceased reporting on this story, no doubt because the editor feared a similar fate.

Luckily, Santa Barbara papers rounded out the historical record. They report that Herrera had fallen in with a gang of rustlers using a forgotten canyon to the west of the city to gather cattle stolen from surrounding ranches. Herrera had for years been using surveying as a way of discovering how best to rob and plunder the state's rich landowners. He must have relished the criminal opportunities in Black Ash Canyon outside of Las Sombras, a swathe of cheap land situated within a day's ride of numerous thriving ranches.

He seems to have gravitated toward the area initially because a relative, one of the many children he had sired out of wedlock during his long career of self-gratification, lived nearby. In the end she turned him into the sheriff's posse, suggesting that Bernardino was no prince among fathers. A gun battle ensued. Herrera and his fellow desperadoes were trapped in a small arroyo branching out from the major canyon. Rather than wait the outlaws out, which might have taken weeks, the posse seized the advantage of favorable winds and set fire to the canyon. Herrera and the other rustlers died of fire or gunfire.

Tolstoy famously asked, "How much land does a man need?" Herrera, like all men, eventually learned the answer. Six feet would do nicely.

The author was writing to sell. His prose went purple here and there. As with the biographical studies of Chambers, his account had been worked up from newspapers and other published sources. I knew better than to look for absolute truth. Writing was never without bias and distortion. The climax of the story had happened a century ago. Everything had fallen into the irretrievable past. No one was left to interview from those days, unless you counted the ghosts.

But the account rang true. I felt I knew Herrera. He came across, and not entirely unsympathetically. Apparently he had shown his father, perhaps a priest as well, some aptitude in mathematics, and been apprenticed to a surveying team. Whatever the backstory, it resulted in a terror-stricken boy standing on a cliff with no choice but to jump. He suffered as a result the lifelong pain and humiliation of his smashed hand. His father's one provision for Bernardino twisted him forever. It gave him his bottomless thirst for revenge. The first of his murdering fires consumed the boys who had driven him to leap from the cliff. From that time on, he became the entitled bastard hell-bent on destroying everything from which he was excluded.

In the end, trapped in Quicksilver Canyon, he met death and revenge in the same guise he had so often handed them out: fire. Once again, as for the ten-year-old chainman, there was only one way out. All lives come down to that. Death is for everyone the one and only way out of the world. Bernardino had jumped as a child. But as the canyon burned, elderly Herrera had, so to speak, clung to the cliff, refusing the one way out, and become a ghost. I knew him all right.

Here was Dieter Thorson's bloodthirsty Chainman, waiting to possess him in Quicksilver Canyon. Here was the vengeful ghost in Valentina's cellar, molding her mind. He was in fact her *grandfather,* though he had never known Valentina in this life. She had come along years after his transformation in Quicksilver Canyon. Between his death and 1960, when Valentina was old enough to be usefully possessed, what was the Herrera spirit doing? He was no doubt haunting the abandoned mercury mine. There might have been early attempts at possession. Herrera the ghost must have slowly matured in strength and daring.

Its motive had again been revenge, a bastard son's revenge on his bastard daughter for the fire that ended his fleshly existence. This was a long, long revenge with no end in sight. Consuela and Angel Acosta, the first known victims, felt Herrera's lurking presence on the edge of their Black Ash Canyon home, and sensed his rage and his power. So they returned as guardian presences, aiming to secure their family's peaceful future. The couple had correctly assessed the danger, but not its power. Valentina, who burned their living flesh in the barn fire, burned their spirits in Old Cabin. Herrera, as a mind-possessing ghost, had ravaged and perverted his granddaughter in order to murder his daughter and son-in-law twice. Twice. That had to be some sort of benchmark in the realm of Hell.

Here was the entity I had at different moments termed Mr. Shadows, the Invader, the Master Ghost, the Inchworm. He mapped and mathematicised my mind. Through Valentina again he tried to burn the cabin where Cheyenne and I slept. On his next visit to my mind he threatened me with the possession of Cheyenne. His mundane existence had been a perfect prelude to a horrifying ghosthood. Long before Bernardino Herrera had been deprived of his physical embodiment, he had been the jealous enemy of life and love. Now he was making ready to corrupt his great-granddaughter.

It was that damn endless recurrence again, the crimes of a father being visited again and again and again, generation after generation after generation, on his heirs.

The King Harkins book had one more gift for me. Among the notes to the eye-opening chapter on Bernardino Herrera was a reference to an essay called "Criminal Surveying During the Benson Years and After" in *Wellsprings: Proceedings of the California Central Coast Historical Association*, Number 25 (1994), pages 52-65. The author was B. Kinsolving. I looked up the journal in the library's online catalog. It had ceased publication in 1995. Through subsequent searches I learned that the Association had only existed for a brief time, from 1982 to 1995, and was based in Goleta. Prof. Jason Hearndon of the Folklore Department at the University of California at Santa Barbara had served as President of the Society and editor of *Wellsprings* until his death in 1995, whereupon the Society and its publication themselves dissolved into the mists of history.

The library held a complete set of the *Wellsprings* journal. Each annual volume contained four issues bound together. But for the year 1993 issue number 25, the one containing the Kinsolving essay, had been ripped out. I could have checked the holdings at other libraries within driving distance, but had no doubt that issue 25 would also be missing from their copies. Someone had tried to erase the Kinsolving piece from the historical record. He had done a good job too. But this self-effacing man was used to recommending books for lazy students. He hadn't counted on my tenacious interest in sources.

Like a fly in my fist, I had him in an outright lie. The teacher had assured me that he knew little about the criminal sides of surveyance. Checking out two of those ghost-hunting manuals that Billy had discussed with us in our first clubhouse meeting, I returned to the Green Pastures.

Good things come in bunches. That evening, while browsing through a discussion of how to expel ghosts from haunted houses, I received a call from Pat Dworkin. A webmaster in Copenhagen admitted that he had received the Thorson notebooks from a customer in 1993 and posted them to his network of anonymity sites, from a few of which they were still available. According to Pat, this webmaster was a famous character in his field, and had once drawn international headlines for refusing to aid in a Danish murder investigation.

"So what did you do, Pat? Put those wizard fingers to work?"

"Yup. I hacked his business files. I had to negotiate several tricky encryption barriers, but I got there. Do you want to write this down?" He gave me the IP address of the computer that had originally sent the notebooks to Denmark. "I did some checking," he continued. "This IP number was issued by Bradley Cable in 1990 to an address in Las Sombras. Get ready to write again." I copied the address. 100 Poplar Valley Lane.

I knew that address. The Auchincloss Academy was there.

I gathered my thoughts in the morning. From the beginning the ghosts had mounted a two-pronged attack. An anthropologist might have called the two fronts "intrafamilial" and "extrafamilial." Valentina, her parents, Cheyenne, myself, were all under siege. But so were innocent girls from outside the family ring. I now had an opportunity to close down this second, extrafamilial attack.

Dieter Thorson had an otherworldly mentor in the ghost of Bernardino Herrera. But he had another, living mentor in Byron Kinsolving. His teacher specialized in helping lonely and disturbed boys. Dieter took the man's independent study unit in survivalism. He learned to make fire, find food, and of course use knives. Dieter's proud discovery that the knife was a better weapon than a gun was a perverse version of survivalist dogma. All the boy had done was shift the interest from minimizing his environmental footprint to minimizing his forensic footprint. Kinsolving told his students ghost stories. Though he lied to me about the matter, he had in fact written an article about criminal surveyors, and I knew from its presence in King Harkins' footnotes that the piece contained material on Bernardino Herrera.

Had the Herrera ghost, perhaps during a camping trip near Black Ash Canyon, sampled the mind of Byron Kinsolving? If he had, I bet he found a man with an appreciation for serial killers, deeply interested in torturing and killing women, but without the stomach for actually doing it. As the proverb went, those who cannot do teach.

To know how to suggest, they also say, is the art of teaching. Kinsolving found promising young men at the Auchincloss Academy and nudged them in the right direction— toward ritual murder, toward Quicksilver Canyon. Pupils of this sort did not come along often. He had posted the notebooks of his first great success, Dieter Thorson. Those notebooks would have been good for recruiting. In the future, it would be a relatively simple matter to give his charges the impression that they had discovered for themselves an unappreciated and enlightening master, with words of wisdom on how best to kill, how to gain strength from a ghostly collaborator, and how to do all of this while living like a proper survivalist. The new serial killer, Dieter Thorson's copycat, must also come from the Kinsolving stable at Auchincloss Academy. There was a good chance that the teacher could be convicted for aiding and abetting the crimes of two murderers. He might even go down on multiple charges of accessory to murder.

I drove to the Las Sombras Sheriff's office and asked to speak to Terry Coleman, the deputy who had interviewed me the morning after Vera Maarten's murder. We spoke for half an hour. Though sceptical and standoffish at first, by the end of our talk he was clearly excited over this new web of connections. I left the ghosts out. I was certain that a thorough investigation of Kinsolving and his current students would be sufficient to bring to an end the budding career of the current Black Ash Canyon Killer.

Putting the Herrera ghost out of commission would be a tougher job. But I had some ideas.

On my way back to the Griswold Ranch I stopped at the graveyard near the entrance to the canyon. I tried to remember the first time I had seen Valentina, standing in the shade behind her palomino, looking down at a headstone. With that image fixed in my mind, I went looking for the grave.

I found it straight off. The area around the grave had been planted with white and pink tea roses. I did not spy a single weed. Valentina tended it well.

The headstone was too new to be the original one. The granddaughter of the grave's supposed occupant must have ordered it herself, once she was mistress of the neighboring ranch. No wonder she confused life with death. This stone was the last confirmation I would need:

### BERNARDINO HERRERA

*mi rey plateado*

*Escapó*

*Escapó*, "escaped." He surely had—not just from life, but from death as well.

CHAPTER ELEVEN

I brought the Ghost Killers up to date on my researches, conclusions, and plans.

Afterward I took Billy aside.

"Listen, Billy. I take it that old boundary dispute with the Griswolds still rankles your father."

"My father isn't well, Mike. But yes, he still finds the energy twice a day to rain down curses on Ben Griswold."

"This may help. I think the Harkins biography of Herrera exposes the backdrop of the feud. Herrera came to the canyon toward the end of his life for three reasons. His daughter Consuela and her husband were squatting on what is now the Griswold Ranch. The canyon was well positioned for thievery. Finally, he landed a surveying job with United Oil to break up their canyon into saleable ranches and farms. Given his longstanding habits, Herrera would have looked around for ways to make an under-the-table profit from that survey. Who was the first owner of the Steele Ranch?"

"Dad bought it from an elderly man named Dinning, I think. Rumor was that he once ran a paddlewheel gambling boat on the Sacramento River."

"Remember the 1915 survey marker we found in Quicksilver Canyon? That must have been left by Herrera's team.

I think Dinning paid Herrera to bump out the eastern boundary of the ranch he intended to buy and give him an extra half mile of Canyon, including two or three oil wells. Who knows?  A kid on the surveying team named Joe Peckham might have noticed the fraud, then said something, assuming it was the result of an error rather than deliberate fraud.  Herrera could have murdered him for his trouble."

Billy uttered the first few notes of a rueful laugh. "Damn.  The whole canyon, every single one of us, is infected.  Amazing how evil spreads in all directions like wildfire."

"Maybe we can replant.  It might quiet your father's mind to know that his phony boundary was the work of a man behind generations of sorrow in the Griswold family. I'll speak to Ben too.  Maybe he and Theo can bury the hatchet before they leave this earth."


A few days after this meeting I received a call from a grateful Terry Coleman.  The Black Ash Canyon Copycat Killer, the new Dieter Thorson, was behind bars.  He turned out to be Paul McCann, the student I dubbed "Wild Child" while waiting to speak to Byron Kinsolving.  He must have been the dark-haired young man, Herrera inside him, who had followed me to the courtyard of the church.  Kinsolving was also in jail. Files on both Thorson and McCann found in the basement of his home were full of incriminating information. He would be charged as an accessory to four murders.

I sat in Valentina Griswold's bedroom, flanked by the rest of the Ghost Killers, speaking with Valentina herself.

"Do you want to be a ghost?"

My question seemed to intrigue her. She paused to think. The ghost was not inside her mental realm now. Valentina appeared more self-possessed than ever before in my presence.

"No. I've done my service. I want to rest."

It was not easy for her to say. Hard-bitten tears flowed from her eyes. I waited till they stopped.

"And you don't really want your daughter to be possessed by him, do you?"

"No."

I had hoped for this response.

"Valentina, I want to hypnotize you so you can think exactly that and fill your entire mind with it. When your grandfather comes to you, I want him to see the strength and conviction in that thought. Otherwise, he will do the wrong things. Do you understand?"

"Yes."

We had arrived at a touchy stage in my plan. I was not a trained hypnotist. Years back I had briefly practiced the art with some friends from college. I looked at my watch. It was 2 AM. Cheyenne thought the ghost usually came through the window around 2:30.

I read in one of the ghost-hunter handbooks that a spirit had to leave a room, a house, or an enclosure by the same route it entered. This dictum was known as the "fundamental rule" of European occultism. Valentina had earlier confirmed this venerable assumption. "Oh yes," she said in response to a direct question on the matter, "you need a nice entrance because he uses it twice."

We expected Herrera to enter at the window. On a table beneath the window we had placed an open cold-forged iron receptacle filled with dirt. It looked like a new indoor window box, but it was actually a carefully baited trap. The dirt was from Bernardino's grave, mixed with some bones from his coffin. According to another ghost-hunter manual I had checked out from the library, dirt from its grave lured a ghost to lie down and rest. It was a logic similar to the coffin and native soil in the vampire myth. The ghost's body had lain in the grave, rotting and dissolving. This was as close as an undead spirit had been to the complete and normal oblivion. It would attract him, encompass him, and if we were fortunate, bewitch him into tarrying there. Ghosts, like human beings, were prone to seek out samples or precursors of non-existence.

I waited a few more minutes, then gave Valentina two Ativan that Cheyenne had earlier fetched from her medicine cabinet. I knew enough about hypnotism to realize that a good tranquilizer would smooth the way. Then I began the standard rigmarole of concentrating on a flashlight beam and counting slowly backwards from fifty. It worked. When she had sunk into a trance, I gave her clear instructions. She was to think deeply and sincerely about the peace of death. It was the end of worrying, the end of caring, the end of every-thing. When her time came, she wanted it. She wanted peace for Cheyenne as well.

We moved her, fixed on those thoughts, to one side of the double bed. I lay down next to her and began methodi-cally composing my mind. When the time came, I would need to think a sequence of thoughts with unaffected pro-fundity. I calmed myself. I felt how the thoughts settled on my mental landscape. I observed  what other thoughts they bordered on.

"Almost time," Billy said.

The Ghost Killers moved their chairs to the wall opposite the window. I let the mental tension seep away. I waited.

Billy spoke again. "I think he's here."

I was sure Herrera would go to Valentina first. He had been entering that mind for over fifty years, and had come to this room to enter it again. When it was my turn, I wanted him to feel my easiness, my lack of tension. Minutes went by.

In the blink of an eye he was in me, rifling my recent memories.

"*You tracked me.*"

"*I did. And I found how alone you are, Herrera.*"

"*I'm not alone.*"

"*Is Dieter Thorson's spirit still with you? He's finished managing serial killers, as you just learned. Has he vowed to find another puppet? Or has he given up the ghost?*"

No answer came.

"*I have also found how bad you are, Herrera.*"

I thought good and hard, with moral horror, of the way he treated Consuela, his badness as a father. I thought good and hard, with moral horror, of the way he treated Valentina, his badness as a grandfather. Molding her to punish her parents was bottomlessly wicked. I thought by contrast of my own grandfather, Wilbur Buckman, and how at his death I was given a lasting memory image of his peacefulness, sitting quietly in our den. I thought good and hard, with utmost moral horror, of the way Herrera intended to treat Cheyenne, his forthcoming badness as a great-grandfather. I brooded on the outlines of his sin. Though I did not find a use for all the ancient seven, I presented the invader with vehement conclusions about his pride, wrath, envy, greed, and sloth.

"*You cannot sit in judgment on me!*" I felt his contempt, spitting on my thoughts.

"*Yes he can.*" Another spirit, neither Herrera nor me, was using my inner voice. "*He's one of your victims. Of course he gets to sit in judgment on you. Valentina already has. You were just inside her. You know she wants no part of your existence.*"

Who was this? I fought my way out of confusion and switched to the next thought in my planned sequence. It combined the Harkins account of Herrera's formative trauma with the fundamental rule of leaving where you entered.

*There is only one way out. One. You must leave as you entered, but in reverse. Out of nothing we arrive, back to nothing we return. You must jump off the cliff, as you did as a child. You must die.*

I was aware that the new presence, the one who had just spoken, was also thinking this thought, amplifying it. Our authority built and built. It became tremendous, like the climax of a symphony.

I must have passed out momentarily when he left me. I heard scraping noises from the direction of the window. The grogginess passed.

"I think we've got him," Billy said.

"He never made it to the window," Cheyenne said. "He definitely went to the dirt. It soaked up his ectoplasm smoke like a sponge."

I rose from the bed and checked the case. Billy and Solly had put on the top piece and sealed the two halves. The snap locks were all in place. They were tightening steel bands to make the seal entirely secure. We had covered the insides of the container with drawn pentagrams. That was another tip from the manuals. Pentagrams prevented spirits from escaping. Maybe ours were working. Maybe the iron was imprisoning. Maybe the grave soil was irresistible. Maybe Herrera had given up the ghost. But every last one of us believed that we had him in the iron container, at our mercy.

I spoke to the spirit remaining in my mind. "*It's you Grandfather, isn't it? Have you always lived in me?*"

No thoughts uttered themselves. No one made use of my inner voice. Instead I saw the memory image from my childhood of Grandfather's ghost at peace in the stillness of our den. He haunted my depths, living in me, but not in the manner the Herrera ghost had inhabited Valentina. He was not a talker, not controlling. He kept to himself. When the chips were down, though, he backed my play and gave me the strength to capture Bernardino Herrera.


Floodlights illuminated the scene. Solly and I were standing together a few feet from the Fountain of Sorrow. Trucks bearing the logo of Obispo Petroleum, the company Solly owned a big chunk of, were parked around the well. Two of them were tanker trucks full of water. There was an organized chaos of cranes, drill bits, wires and cables. It would not be long.

"So that's what half a million bucks looks like," I said.

"Looks good, doesn't it?" Solly answered. "We bored a hundred feet down, then began drilling horizontally on a beeline for the mercury mine in Quicksilver Canyon. I think we hit it on the button. Yesterday I went over to the canyon, then had the boys blow fifty gallons of water and sand through the hole. There was a tremor in exactly the right place. I predict we are right underneath the mine. That sulphur lake in the center is going to flush like a toilet." Music to my ears. The focus of our project was the collapsed tunnels behind and beneath the old mercury mine. When we tripped that ghost macro, or whatever it was, a shadow-gathered figure introduced the back of the mine as if certain death waited there. None of us doubted that it did. Billy called the entrance a portal leading from this world to noth-ingness. Herrera had lived near this gateway for many years. He knew its meaning.

We intended to attack the old mine from below. The tunnels would implode. Millions of tiny fissures would open, draining its filthy waters. The Herrera ghost, his bones, and the soil from his former grave would mingle in this process, and all of them in the end would lie dispersed in the geologi-cal skeleton of Quicksilver Canyon.


Near dawn I walked over to the centerpiece of our plans, and put my hand on the iron canister. Herrera invaded me again. Perhaps the iron muffled him or the pentagrams restrained him. But he seemed to be weakened, and got no further than the threshold of my mind.  "*I will not die*," he told me.

"*Yes you will*," I replied. "*It's your time to leave.  Good-bye, Herrera.*"

As I walked away, the ghost slipped from my mind as gently as an abandoned thought.  I was glad to know for sure that we had captured him.


By mid-morning we were ready.  Our crew went into action.  At the driller's order the projectile glided down the borehole to the juncture where the horizontal shaft turned back up toward the surface.  The motorman pumped in a hundred gallons of pressurized water.  Just as our iron torpedo was about to get crunched around, we hit the remote control that detonated its small explosive.  The earth shook a little.  Then the motorman rammed down a ton of pressurized water and sand with a few chemical lubricants to smooth the way.  The earth shook more than a little.

For a moment we stood around, frozen, as if waiting for sirens to wail or a ghost to counterattack.  There was nothing but silence.  We returned to life.  Solly and Billy began dancing around, exulting.

"We *fracked* that sonofabitch!" Billy whooped. "Wait till the paranormalists hear about this! We'll be legends! I know it cost a fortune, Mike, but was it worth it? Hell yes, for damn sure yes. Bring on the fines. He's been powdered! Pulverized! Whatever that thing was made of, and it had to be made of something, it's dribbling through millions of new pockets and passageways in the bedrock."

"That was beautiful! That was beautiful! That was beautiful!" Solly crowed. "That was no raindrops are falling on my head type deal. Sucker never knew what hit him! Fracked over once and for all! Sayonara and rest in peace, asshole."

Life had won.

We had a party at the clubhouse with big tin tubs of ice-cooled beers, hard ciders, and white wines. At the end of the evening, having said goodnight to our drilling crew, we Ghost Killers turned off the music and sat around enjoying our nightcaps of choice.

"One thing I really don't understand," I said to my friends, "is why this started a couple of weeks ago. Why did the Herrera ghost, who seemed to be operating successfully from Quicksilver Canyon, suddenly demand to take over Old

Cabin? Why did the spirits of Angel and Consuela, right then and there, have to go?"

"I think that's an easy one," Billy said. "It was you, Mike—your arrival in the canyon. You changed everything. You were exactly the man for Cheyenne. Valentina knew it. Herrera knew it. Shy would never belong to him the way Valentina had. Angel Acosta had managed to contact you and place messages in your writing. You were ghost-sensitive, ghost-friendly if you want, and you would never be won over to Herrera's pathetic vengeances. Before you took Cheyenne away, before your full powers were known, he had to act."

I was still puzzled. "Why did Valentina, presumably under Herrera's power, set fire to my cabin when both Cheyenne and I were sleeping inside?"

Our leader had an answer for that too. "She came in the early morning, not the dead of night. That fire was probably started in the hope of scaring you off. But I do think the ghost knew in some manner that you were capable of killing it. That's why he tried with desperate threats to prevent you from learning his history. His deepest wish was to separate you and Cheyenne. But had the opportunity presented itself to kill you at the price of killing Cheyenne, I bet he would reluctantly have taken the deal. We destroyed him—you destroyed him—before that opportunity arose."

Billy slapped me on the shoulder. Solly was nodding. Cheyenne was smiling and nodding. I felt a deep sigh of approval. It might have been Grandfather. Everyone seemed to agree that I had found the place I belonged.

www.ingramcontent.com/pod-product-compliance
Lightning Source LLC
Chambersburg PA
CBHW071502170626
46811CB00007B/2684